# *A Country Parish*
## *'Christmas'*

# *Mistletoe & Mayhem*

**A Country Parish Christmas: Mistletoe and Mayhem**

© 2025 James Thomas

All rights reserved. The author prohibits anyone from reproducing, storing in a retrieval system, or transmitting any part of this publication in any form or by any means—electronic, mechanical, photocopying, recording, or otherwise—without prior written permission, except for brief quotations used in reviews or critical articles.

This is a work of fiction. The author's imagination has created the names, characters, places, and incidents, or the author used them fictitiously. Any resemblance to actual persons, living or dead, or actual events, is coincidental.

**First published in the United Kingdom, 2025**
by James Thomas

Cover design © James Thomas 2025
ISBN 9798272839831

For information, permissions, or to contact the author:
**www.jthomasbooks.co.uk**

Printed and bound in the United Kingdom

***Dedication***
*For everyone who's ever sung the wrong verse, overcooked the sprouts, or tried to keep the peace at Christmas —*

*You are the genuine miracle.*

— **James Thomas**

# Cast of Characters

*(In order of appearance, interference, or sheer persistence.)*

## Canon David Thomlinson
Vicar of St Michael's, he's thoughtful, kind, and only in control of his parish. He means to preach *"Truth beneath the tinsel,"* but ends up tangled in it instead.

## Mrs Elizabeth Ashdown
Queen of Ashdown Hall. Elegant, commanding, and gloriously indiscreet. Runs the parish's social life as if it were foreign policy, with charm as her chosen weapon.

## Charlotte Bennett
Elizabeth's patient secretary and the quiet engine of order behind every triumph and disaster. Practical, loyal, and perpetually two steps behind chaos.

## Mrs Elinor Dawson
Self-appointed guardian of parish morals and master of useful information. Married to the choirmaster, but emotionally wedded to administration.

## Mr Gerald Davies
Choirmaster, mild-mannered husband, and permanent casualty of his wife's efficiency. Finds solace in hymn tunes and crosswords.

## David Wills
Tower-captain and lord of the bell ringers. Loud, loyal, and convinced he's in charge.

## Beryl Wills
His sharper-tongued, steadier half. Knows every rumour before it's cooled and enjoys them like seasonal pudding.

## Montague Wraxall-Blythe
Organist, dramatist, and self-declared visionary. He believes that smoke, sequins, or philosophy, or ideally all three, can improve all events.

## Daisy Rivers
Young seamstress and choir member; gentle, hopeful, and occasionally the village's conscience. Finds herself in the middle of gossip she never earned.

## Mr Perkins
Builder, reluctant Joseph, and occasional donkey. He is perpetually miscast in timely instances.

## The Barlow's
A well-meaning couple who contribute eagerly to parish opinions.

## The Bartletts
A long-established village family, always ready with advice.

## Villagers, Bells & Choir
Murmuring, meddling, baking, the chorus of St Michael's bears witness.

## Mitre the Cat
Unbothered, and usually asleep in the crib.

## The Cufflinks (D & E)
Old-gold, elegantly engraved, endlessly mislaid. A pair of tiny witnesses to love, gossip, and grace.

*Every village needs a cast. St Michael's simply insists on an encore.*

## Welcome to St Michael's

Somewhere between the sea and the motorway, where the map forgets to be ambitious, lies the village of St Michael's. From a distance it looks exactly as an English village should: slate roofs, curling chimneys, and a church tower doing its best impression of moral authority.

Closer inspection reveals the truth, which is, as always, more entertaining.

The pub doubles as a debating chamber. The choir doubles as a social experiment. The bell ringers ring as if salvation depends on decibels, and the Parochial Church Council meets mainly to prove that democracy can, in fact, be weaponised.

At the heart of it all stands Canon David Thomlinson, a man of faith, patience, and occasional regret. His sermons are famous for being both shorter and more coherent than his meetings. His congregation cherishes him, although in different manners or at diverse intervals.

The grande dame of the district, Mrs Elizabeth Ashdown of Ashdown Hall, presides over the social order with a diamond smile and the air of someone perpetually disappointed in other people's curtains. Her assistant, Charlotte Bennett, ensures the house (and her employer) never entirely combust.

Daisy Rivers, the village's unofficial optimist, keeps the choir in tune and everyone else in hope. Montague, organist, dramatist, and occasional heretic, provides the necessary mischief. Mrs Elinor Dawson, whose opinions are both numerous and well distributed, ensures the rest of the community never grows complacent.

Together, they form a parish that cannot agree on hymn numbers, politics, or how to pronounce *Amen*, but somehow manages to agree on love, or at least on forgiveness, which is the next best thing.

It is a place where gossip travels faster than grace, but grace still wins through persistence. Where miracles are often mistaken for administrative oversights, and where every Christmas brings both catastrophe and clarity in roughly equal measure.

The world rarely notices St Michael's. That's how the village likes it. It keeps the scandals smaller, the friendships stronger, and the glitter (mostly) inside the church.

So, if you find yourself passing through, stay for Evensong, mind the bell tower, and never underestimate the power of tea, tinsel, and second chances.

Welcome to St Michael's, where faith is frequently misplaced, but is always found again, usually in time for Christmas.

# Chapter One
## The Invitation Arrives

Frost glazed St Michael's like spun sugar, prettifying even the bins behind the Red Lion and the noticeboard whose top sheet still pleaded for volunteers for *Pilates for the Over, Ebullient*. White ruffs were on the yews, and the lychgate creaked, possibly signalling there would be a complaint letter from the Barlow's. From the rise above, Ashdown Hall surveyed the village the way a duchess inspects the pews, affectionately, but with standards.

At the breakfast table, Elizabeth Ashdown was engaged in her favourite sport: refinement disguised as generosity. "Charlotte," she said, eyes on a stack of proofs, "if the stationer insists on using robin-red envelopes, he must print addresses in black. Scarlet on scarlet is for admirers and unpaid bills."

Charlotte Penry, long-suffering, twenty-nine, immaculate even under siege, made a note. "Noted, Mrs Ashdown."

"Remove the word 'gala.' A gala is what people have when they can't afford a Ball. We are having a Ball." She tapped the thick cream cards spread across the linen. The Ashdown crest was embossed so sharply one could shave with it. Beneath, in italic propriety:

*You are cordially invited to the Ashdown Christmas Ball.*

*Carols, Champagne & Charity Raffle.*

*Black Tie, Good Sense Optional.*

Elizabeth spread marmalade with surgical precision. "Add, 'Mistletoe supplied at reasonable intervals.' We mustn't pretend we're above horticulture. And ensure Canon David receives his by hand. If one sends a vicar anything by post, it arrives at Epiphany smelling faintly of incense and apology."

Charlotte tucked a strand of hair behind her ear. "The stationer delivered two boxes: invitations, and personal Christmas cards. But there was a labelling... moment."

Elizabeth looked up. "A moment?"

"He wasn't certain which box contained which."

"Charlotte, darling," Elizabeth said, rising, "top-layer checking is for optimists and brides. Unpack them all before the village does. And confirm the raffle licence. I refuse to be audited by the PCC between pudding and cheese on Boxing Day."

The house, like its mistress, looked effortless until you bothered to count the moving parts. Mrs Trevelyan, the housekeeper, supervised with the quiet fatalism of a woman who had seen three rectors come and go and all their cookery. Outside, Owen the gardener was attempting to coax the illuminated reindeer into standing without appearing intoxicated. In the back drive, the caterers' van breathed steam and intention. Somewhere upstairs, two bedrooms were being aired that would not, in the end, be slept in. Alexandra and Henry, Elizabeth's grown up children, were apparently *with friends* for the holidays. In Ashdown usage, this meant London, work, and a choreography of promising texts that never quite ripened into arrivals.

Elizabeth glanced at her phone and then away from it with practised indifference. "If either of my offspring phone," she said to Charlotte, "tell them I am flourishing and not to worry about the speeches. I shall be brief and memorable."

"You are never both," Charlotte murmured, and received one of those looks which meant she had pleased her employer by being impertinent.

Across the valley, Canon David Thomlinson's study smelt of candle wax and resigned faith. The radiator emitted the sort of heat that mocked belief in miracles. A single pane was etched with ferns of frost, and through it the Ashdown house sat on its hill like a smug Christmas cake. He was circling his sermon theme, *Truth beneath the tinsel*, but each draft veered either toward scolding or sentimentality. He desired simplicity, to speak softly, point to a manger, let people hear their own unvarnished hearts. He had known parishes that lived on doctrine and others that lived on drama; St Michael's had taken a sensible decision to do both.

A knock interrupted him. "Come in," he called, expecting Mrs Dawson with choir lists or possibly a complaint about shepherds' tea-lights violating seventeen fire codes. Instead, the postman appeared, pink-cheeked and burdened with a box the size of a font. "For you, Vicar. Fragile. Looks like trouble."

On the lid: *From Ashdown Hall*. Inside, an orderly snowdrift of cream envelopes and, tucked among them, a slim parcel wrapped in midnight paper with an insolent satin bow. The tag read: *For E.A., with all my love — M.*

"I don't imagine I'm E.A.," said David.

"Unless you've taken to initials," said the postman. "It's fashionable." He produced a second envelope addressed to *Canon David Thomlinson (and guest)* in Elizabeth's firm hand. "That one's definitely you. Also, Mr Perkins wanted me to ask whether fake geese count as livestock for the hall hire deposit."

"Tell Mr Perkins that the Lord's mercies are new every morning," said David, "and the church's patience less so." He glanced at the lid again, Invitations, Parish Distribution; and sighed. "Better not send them back. If I don't deliver them, Mrs Ashdown will sense hesitation from her drawing room."

The postman grinned. "She does have a way. Merry early Christmas, Vicar."

When the door closed, David held his invitation to the light. Mistletoe supplied at reasonable intervals. Elizabeth always did like vice with a timetable. He slid the card beneath his paperweight, a smooth beach stone from a summer he rarely mentioned, and scribbled a note: Truth under glitter; God chooses barns, people choose baubles. Meet them gently where they are. He underlined gently twice.

The morning did that village thing of lengthening as it went along because everybody was telling everyone else something urgent. In Dawson's Stores, where the oranges leaned like moral examples and the sweets were arranged so piously they might have been for confession, Mrs Elinor Dawson arranged hymn sheets and information. She collected facts the way others collected stamps, tidily; then weaponized them. When she spotted Charlotte outside with a bulging tote of envelopes, she flung open the door as if rescuing a kitten.

"Oh, my dear, are those what I think they are?"

"Invitations," Charlotte panted. "And Mrs Ashdown's personal cards. There was a labelling issue."

"Labels," said Mrs Dawson, "are civilisation's hinges. Without them, my Gerald would be wearing the dog's flea treatment as aftershave." She plucked an envelope with the tact of a cat. "I'll see these reach the choir."

"If you wouldn't mind," Charlotte said, half relieved, half terrified. "And please, the champagne references are metaphorical."

"My love," said Mrs Dawson, "in this choir, everything except gossip is metaphorical." Her sharp eyes caught a cluster of red, gold, edged envelopes. "And these?"

"Mrs Ashdown's personal cards," said Charlotte quickly. "Please don't mix…"

"Darling, I've never mixed anything except a trifle." She swept off with the bag, virtue in motion, and Charlotte stood a moment in the doorway practising breathing.

Behind the counter, Mr Gerald Davies looked up from counting change and mercy. "Elinor, have you borrowed the vicar's newspaper again?"

"If he prefers the crossword blank, he should rise earlier," she replied, and vanished toward the church with the air of a woman improving a situation.

Down the lane, the bakery's doorbell pinged like a hopeful soul. Anwen Hughes, who baked as if absolution could be achieved with butter, was arranging mince pies the size of decisions. In the queue, Arthur Preece, retired, opinionated, twinkling, held forth to Megan Lewis, the youngest of the bell ringers, whose hair was the colour of new pennies and whose patience was heroic.

"He puts too much sermon in the sermon," Arthur said. "I prefer the old style. Less theology, more telling off."

"I like it when he's kind," Megan said. "Makes it feel like we might be, too."

"Young people," said Arthur, satisfied, and ordered a Chelsea bun as if it had disagreed with him.

Tom Evans, landlord of the Red Lion, lugged in a crate of oranges and a rumour. "Ashdown's doing a Ball," he announced, in the tone of a man breaking a drought. "I'm making a cocktail called *Roof Appeal*. It'll be mostly gin and repentance."

"Put it on the chalkboard," said Anwen. "People like to know what's going to happen to them."

By the time the buns were selected and the queue had decided the weather was really very brave, the invitations had acquired a sort of molecular life. Mrs Dawson's tote bag sagged heroically as she delivered by hand, inserting judgement when stamps would have sufficed. She stopped at the post office because duty required that she be seen to be doing duty, and was rewarded by the queue's reverent curiosity. The postmaster, who had the face of a man who had read all human mail and remained loyal to civilisation, tilted an eyebrow. "Busy, Mrs D?"

"Public service," she said. "We are all of us called."

Behind her, the Barlow's murmured something about whether black tie meant actually black. The Bartletts countered with a view on cummerbunds. A teenager in a bobble hat Googled "What is a cummerbund?" and looked at the results as if they were a dare.

In the tower chamber, which smelt permanently of oak dust, rope and denial, David Wills, captain of bells and bluster, addressed his troop. "Right, lovelies. Quarter peal of Grandsire for Christmas Eve, provided Beryl keeps time instead of opinions."

Beryl, wrapped in a tartan scarf capable of sheltering livestock, sniffed. "If you'd listen, David, my opinions might improve your backstroke." Laughter fluttered around the ropes. On the windowsill, a box read *Mulled Wine, Donation from the Red Lion (Do Not Test)*. Someone had tested.

"And the party," David Wills went on. "Fewer spillages. No removing clappers for comedy. Last year's stunt nearly deafened the curate."

"We haven't got a curate," said Megan.

"Exactly," said David. "He never recovered from the interview."

Montague the local hazard, raised a tinsel, decorated hand. "I have an idea to delight and unite..."

"No quiz, Monty," said Beryl. "Last time you asked, 'Name three composers who died on Tuesdays' you were the only one who cared."

"This is theatre!" cried Montague. "The parish thirsts for art."

"Let it drink cocoa," said Beryl. "And bring sausage rolls."

"Actually," said Megan, "I could make sausage rolls."

Beryl eyed her approvingly. "Talent. At last."

Word moved through the village like light through stained glass—bent, beautified, slightly discoloured. At Raven Cottage, Daisy Rivers, needlewoman, second soprano, possessor of dimples considered local landmarks, turned her envelope over twice, wondering if a certain someone read his at that very moment. She propped the card on the mantel beside a pale watercolour of the church and told herself not to be ridiculous. In the Red Lion, Tom chalked *Ashdown Ball Cocktails* on the board and began marinating oranges in optimism. At No. 3 Forge Cottages, Mr Perkins, builder, reluctant Joseph, occasional donkey, examined a crate of plastic geese and decided that if they were livestock, they were very brave livestock indeed.

In his study, Canon David fought his sermon again. God does not insist you be dazzling, he wrote. Only honest; the manger's straw scratches everyone equally. He frowned. Perhaps too agricultural. He stood, stretched, and persuaded the radiator to confess heat. The village produced sounds like a clock that had decided to be festive: a trumpet attempting *O Come, All Ye Faithful* with noble failure; a child announcing to the street that snow was edible; a dog offering a commentary on the child's methodology.

A knock on the window startled him. Elizabeth Ashdown stood outside, coat swirling like a verdict. He opened the door.

"Canon," she said, stepping in with the fragrance of wool, perfume, and authority, "a personal delivery. The post is charming in theory and deplorable in practice."

"I've already received the crate," he said. "I suspect…"

"Ah yes, the box." She smiled thinly. "Charlotte tells me the stationer's lapse may have... blossomed. If any of my Christmas cards appear among the invitations, please retrieve them. They contain family photographs. Nothing short of scandal."

"Worse," he said. "Documentation."

"Exactly. Return any strays with all discretion. And no judging."

"Not judging is my side of the street," he said. "Though people like to peer over the hedge."

"Let them. Idleness must feed on something between Advent and Lent." She hesitated, a rare crack of candour. "You'll preach truth again this year, won't you? You always do when the lights are at their fairy-est."

"I try."

"Be kind with it," she said softly. "Some of us are held together by a thread."

"Always."

"Do come to the Ball, bring a guest or at least your good sense. We're raffling to raise money for the church roof. I've put Montague on tickets; it keeps him from the piano."

"Bless you. If you stop him adding descants, we might achieve peace on earth."

"Peace on earth is dull," she said. "I'll settle for entertainment with a conscience."

Her gaze roamed over the study—the books stacked like arguments, the salvaged chair, the beach stone under which he put things he couldn't say out loud. Her late husband had once stood here and explained to David why the church roof leaked in ways that defied physics but not cost. That had been the summer before the illness, when everyone had thought time was a promise. She looked away. "I must go and supervise a star that refuses to behave."

"I shall pray for it," he said.

"Pray for Mr Perkins," she replied. "He's under it."

When she'd gone, the room seemed to hum with her after-presence. He put on his coat and stepped into the snow. The village hall was inevitably alight. Through its windows spilled laughter and lunacy. Inside, painted scenery, a crate of plastic geese and, inexplicably, a vast silver star on wheels. Montague, in shirtsleeves and fervour, directed three choir ladies pretending to be ducks. "And then," he proclaimed, "the vicar says, 'Peace on earth!' and the Fairy Godmother replies, 'Not if I can help it!' and we...oh." He froze. "Canon! We were...this is...".

"A health and safety audit," said Mrs Dawson, appearing from behind a curtain with a clipboard that had clearly just materialised. "Entirely routine. Tinsel compliance."

David eyed the scene. "That's a very assertive star."

"It's for the climactic reveal," Montague said.

"Of what?"

"Hope," said Montague solemnly. "And possibly Mr Perkins in a leotard. Negotiations ongoing."

Mr Perkins, who had been promoted to donkey in a moment of weakness, saluted sheepishly and then tried to look like a moral lesson. Daisy was pinning a hem with brisk care; Megan hovered, offering straight pins like cavalry.

"I'm all for hope," David said. "Just keep it from rolling into the nave during the second lesson."

"Of course," said Mrs Dawson. "We wouldn't upstage the Word with Tada."

He left them to it and walked home through the soft snow. Lights pricked behind frosted panes. A silhouette lifted a child to see the star that wasn't supposed to be there yet. Somewhere a radio offered a recording of King's (The annual Christmas Eve service from King's College Chapel, famous for its choir and the opening solo of *Once in Royal David's City*) and lost bravely to frying onions. The courage of it, the ordinary holiness of people still trying, warmed him more than the thin air ever could.

Back at the vicarage, his doormat had acquired an air of theatre. A final envelope waited: deep red, gold, edged, sealed with the Ashdown crest. Inside, a short note and a small velvet box.

Canon. *This is clearly not meant for me, though it found me. The stationer's "moment" appears to have become a season. Please deliver it to its rightful owner before the ball. Discretion required; drama inevitable. E.*

He opened the box and found a pair of old-gold cufflinks engraved with two intertwined letters: D and E. He shut the lid carefully, the way one closes a remark that could ruin a dinner. There were at least three pairs of initials those could belong to—David and Elinor (God forbid), Derek and Elaine (they were barely on speaking terms), or the pairing the village would choose even if time itself objected. He placed the box beside his sermon notes and added one last line: If love is messy at Christmas, it's because God trusted us with it.

Outside, a single bell tolled, once, twice, reconsidered, and tolled again. Mitre the Cat installed itself in the crib with a theological sigh. Up at the Hall, a reindeer lurched into dignity, and Elizabeth, at a window no one could see into, tried very hard not to look at her phone. Across the lanes, Charlotte drafted a list of contingencies and then drafted a list of contingencies for the contingencies, because experience had taught her that St Michael's, given half a chance, preferred to be interesting. And down at the Red Lion, Tom Evans wrote *Roof Appeal* in chalk letters so large that even repentance would see them, and told the room in general that he'd always liked a church with ambition.

The frost thickened, and the village tucked itself into its routines like hands into pockets, ringing practice and panto, puddings and polish, rumours and resolutions, each one stitched to the next by a thread no one could see but everyone felt: the knowledge that, sooner or later, they would all have to be in the same room, singing the same song, pretending they didn't mind. And above it all, the bell, slightly wrong, cheerfully persistent, kept time for people who would never keep it for themselves.

## Chapter Two
## The Wrong Cards

By morning, the frost had settled in with a sense of permanence, as if the village had been lacquered overnight. Chimneys smoked, sparrows skittered like rumours, and somewhere a radio sang that it was beginning to look a lot like…well, St Michael's always looked like that, it simply tried harder in December.

Charlotte Penry arrived at Ashdown Hall before nine, crisp as a list. The front steps had been salted into submission; Owen, the gardener, stood contemplating an ice-slick reindeer with the fatalism of a man who knew it would fall again the moment he turned his back. In the morning room, sunlight pooled on the rugs and lit the ranked invitations like an army of cream-coloured soldiers.

Elizabeth was already awake and weaponized. She wore a pale sweater and the expression of a woman who could host an ambassadorial crisis over toast. "Report," she said.

"Two boxes completely unpacked," Charlotte answered, setting down her bag and opening her notebook. "Invitations confirmed, cards mostly separated, minor casualties among the envelopes. I've instructed Mrs Trevelyan to reserve the library for the raffle-prize staging area. The florist rang. She says 'tasteful' or 'triumphal' for the staircase?"

"'Tasteful,' because I'm not. Situation with the labelling?"

"Rescuable, but..." Charlotte hesitated. "Mrs Dawson may have... assisted."

Elizabeth's spoon paused in her yoghurt. "Assisted—the verb that has ruined nations."

"She took a bag to 'speed distribution.' I did try to stop her."

"My dear, no one stops Elinor Dawson. One merely gets out of her way and claims destiny later." Elizabeth crossed to the window, where the house's view made the church look flattering. "We must assume some invitations are now nestled inside my personal Christmas cards, and some Christmas cards have been delivered to the deserving, the innocent, and the unready."

"Shall I ring the vicarage?" Charlotte asked. "Or will that simply persuade him that we've escalated to a military alert?"

"Both are true. Ring him, then tell Mrs Dawson we're deeply grateful and would like the remainder of the bag, the tote, and her soul back."

While Charlotte went in search of a signal, the rest of the village was already fermenting. The post,office queue had lengthened into a society; the bakery's bell pinged itself hoarse. At Dawson's Stores, Mrs Elinor Dawson stood at the centre of her web like a benevolent spider armed with sheet music.

"You can't fault me for efficiency," she told Anwen Hughes, who had brought in a basket of stollen so fragrant it constituted coercion.

"Civic duty is it?" said Anwen. "Is that what we call gossip now?"

"Gossip is what idle people do. I curate information." She lowered her voice to a pitch that suggested choirs and revelations. "Between ourselves, the vicar has already received two of Elizabeth's personal Christmas cards. The ones with...well. Family references."

Anwen's eyebrows climbed. "Photographs?"

"I said nothing."

"You said everything."

Mrs Dawson smiled beatifically and adjusted her pile of carol sheets. "I expect him to issue a dignified statement at Matins."

"About photographs?"

"About truth," Mrs Dawson said, and looked as if she had invented the concept.

Two doors down, at the Blackbird Bakery, Arthur Preece monopolised the corner table, tutting affectionately at the state of the jam tarts. "Crust too neat," he told Megan Lewis, who had come in for hot chocolate and a thaw. "Makes you suspicious."

"You're suspicious of everything," Megan said. "It's your charm."

"It's my contribution," Arthur said. "The modern world needs more suspicion and better mince pies. Did you hear the vicar's been sent something from Ashdown? And not a bill."

Megan rolled her eyes. "He gets sent lots of things. People think he has time."

"Doesn't he?"

"No," she said firmly, and paid for her drink with coins that had been felted by the cold.

Canon David Thomlinson was not thinking about photographs. He was thinking about paper cuts. A second, smaller box had arrived by breakfast; the parish had an appetite for stationery that would have alarmed a less stubborn priest. He had already sorted by street and by family, and had reached the philosophical stage of distribution where one considered whether the Almighty had intended the world to possess so many Barlow's.

When the doorbell rang with a flurry that sounded like guilt, he opened it to find Charlotte on the step, cheeks varnished with cold and mortification. She looked like efficiency mid-faint.

"Canon," she said, "we have a problem of the sort that prefers to be called an opportunity for growth."

"Come in," he said, stepping back before she could reconsider existence.

In the kitchen she explained: the crates, the lapse, the tote bag, the village's talent for reading italics. He listened, made coffee, and kept his face in that pastoral setting he saved for funerals and budgets.

"And in conclusion," Charlotte said, hands wrapped around the mug, "I'm so sorry."

"In conclusion," he said gently, "this is one of those parish situations in which no one has died and therefore everything is survivable." He poured himself a mercy. "What precisely was on these personal Christmas cards?"

"Photographs," she admitted. "Not disgraceful, awkward. The family at the Hall last Christmas, Mrs Ashdown, her late husband, the children. There's a note."

"Ah," he said, carefully not asking about the note. "Well, our small village loves a mystery. It loves two mysteries even more. We already had the cufflinks…"

"The what?"

He gestured towards the study. "A pair of old-gold cufflinks that seem to have migrated via Ashdown into my life. Initials D and E. Unhelpful."

Charlotte blinked, calculating initials and outcomes. "Oh dear."

"Oh dear," he agreed. "In the short term, can we prevent further distribution?"

"I'll persuade Mrs Dawson that the choir needs her tactical oversight. That should keep her still long enough to undo the damage she hasn't yet done."

"Mobilise the music," he said. "A time-honoured method."

"Mrs Ashdown will apologise, but not too much."

"Good. We are Anglican. Excess apology looks Catholic."

She laughed, the colour returning to her face.

By eleven, the invitations and card mis-deliveries had generated their own weather system. Children ran messages that bore only a family resemblance to the originals. At the Red Lion, Tom Evans designed a lunchtime special called *The Mistletoe,* which was three parts fizz and one part regret. At the post office, a woman in a purple coat demanded to know whether black tie allowed tartan, and the postmaster replied with the gravity of a judge that tartan had been allowed since 1746 and possibly a week before.

Mrs Dawson, hijacked by Charlotte's claim of a "choir emergency," convened an impromptu rehearsal at the church. "We have been accused," she informed the altos, "of under-ambition. Our descants must be robust without vulgarity."

"Vulgarity is Monty's department," Beryl Wills observed, toeing off snow. "He's rewriting the organ voluntarily; that alone is suspicious."

Gerald Davies propped the vestry door on a hymn book and whispered to David, "We're merely tiring her out."

"Thank you," David said. "If she runs out of energy before Evensong, we may preserve civilisation."

He made two rounds through the pews, handing out invitations to people who had already received them but wanted the vicar's copy as a keepsake. In Row Four, Arthur Preece squinted at his card. "It says '*and guest.*' Is that binding?"

"Not sacramentally."

"I was thinking of asking my rheumatism. It goes everywhere with me."

In the side aisle, Daisy Rivers arranged holly in a brass pot with the concentration of someone daring fate to flirt with her again. She looked up as David passed and their hellos bumped and blushed like teenagers. "Nice morning," she said.

"Hypothetically," he replied, and the code of the conversation, that they were both pretending to be unremarkable, held fast.

By noon Charlotte had reappeared at the Hall, victorious, with Mrs Dawson's tote bag half recovered and promises obtained under the guise of rehearsal. Elizabeth accepted the bag as if it contained a small bomb. "Damage?"

"Containable," Charlotte said. "It's mostly speculation fuel."

"I prefer wood," Elizabeth said. "Speculation smokes." She riffled a fresh list. "What is Tom Evans calling his new cocktail?"

"'*The Mistletoe.*' He's also offering a '*Roof Appeal.*'"

"Good man. Everyone should feel involved."

Mrs Trevelyan entered with the calm of a woman who had seen the Queen and the plumbing on the same day. "The charity-raffle items have begun to arrive," she said. "A hamper, a spa voucher, a ceramic hedgehog of indeterminate function, and Mr Perkins's geese."

"The geese are not a raffle prize," Charlotte said quickly. "They're scenery."

"I am relieved," said Mrs Trevelyan, and went away to be practical elsewhere.

Elizabeth turned back to the window where the lawn was performing a dress rehearsal of winter. "Should we mind that the village believes I'm sending the vicar personal notes and heirlooms?"

"Would you mind?" Charlotte asked.

Elizabeth considered. "It lends a certain glamour to my day. But we mustn't ruin his. He is fragile in the manner of men who believe they are not."

"Then we'll correct it, gently."

"Gently," Elizabeth echoed, testing whether the word would pass her lips without complaint. Her phone buzzed, blinked once with the world beyond the valley, and fell silent again. She did not look at it.

After lunch, the bell ringers gathered in the Red Lion for what they called *"coordination"* and everyone else called *loudly*. Megan Lewis arrived with a Tupperware box and was greeted as if she had smuggled a saint. "Sausage rolls," Beryl announced, opening the lid and blessing them. "Proper ones. Not those nervous supermarket twigs."

Montague appeared from a cloud of cologne, tapping the chalkboard with a long finger. "Observe: a signature drink. This will uplift our party and our hearts."

Tom Evans polished a glass. "It will lift the carpet. What's that glitter on your sleeve, Monty?"

"Art," Montague said. "Possibly on loan from the school. Did you hear about the cards?"

"Only that half the village has been invited to the wrong thing," Tom said. "Which is to say, the right thing."

"Delicious," Montague sighed. "I do so enjoy an unforced error."

"Then you'll love what's coming," Beryl muttered.

At three, with light beginning to fade, the village hall shook itself out like a theatre cat. The pantomime troupe had been promised an hour *"without pyrotechnics,"* which Montague had chosen to interpret as *"with ambition."* The silver star had recovered from yesterday's crisis and now rolled obediently when prodded with a broom handle.

"Places for the angelic announcement," Mrs Dawson called, clipboard restored to sovereignty. "Daisy, wand upright, dignity of heaven. Mr Perkins, you are a donkey, not a commentary; Montague; lamentably, you are a villain."

"I prefer antagonist," Montague said, smoothing his velvet lapel.

"Antagonise quietly," Mrs Dawson replied.

They ran the scene, lost the wand, found the wand, found a second wand that no one recalled ordering, and negotiated with the star, which had developed opinions. During a pause for sanity, Daisy stepped into the corridor for water and found the vicar there, removing a stray bit of tinsel from his sleeve with an expression of pastoral resignation.

"Oh," she said, startled. "You're here."

"I'm everywhere," he said mildly. "It's my spiritual brand."

She laughed, then sobered. "I'm sorry about the cards. People are awful."

"People are splendid," he said. "They're simply not good at secrets."

"I mean you," she said, flushing. "The rumours. They're not fair."

He tilted his head. "We live in a village. Fair is a springtime vegetable. It arrives late and leaves early."

"You make it sound manageable."

"Everything is until it isn't. Then we panic and call it tradition."

She smiled, that tenderness in her eyes that had nothing to do with him and everything to do with the world. Somewhere behind them Montague shouted "Tread softer! You are trampling symbolism," and they returned to the hall, where symbolism allowed itself to be trampled with only minor protest.

By four o'clock, the hour when even gossip takes tea, a kind of afternoon truce had descended: Elizabeth used it to visit the church with a basket of ribbon and the air of a duchess visiting a colony. Charlotte trailed with a list and a pencil that could be used as a weapon.

"Canon," Elizabeth called softly at the porch, where David was inspecting a notice about fire exits that had been written by someone who distrusted exits. "We have come to apologise."

"Excellent," he said. "We're rationing those."

"It was all my fault," she went on, with a precision that suggested she would accept responsibility for the Great Fire of London if it speeded things up. "The stationer had a moment. I compounded the moment by existing; Mrs Dawson did her duty and made matters worse. We shall correct it. You are not," she added, "the subject of my family Christmas."

"Then the village will be disobliged," he said. "It's been having such a lovely time."

She smiled, eyes glinting. "Let them. Idleness likes a bone."

"Thank you," he said, and meant it. "Charlotte, thank you for your diplomacy."

Charlotte inclined her head with the modesty of a woman who had wrangled both a choir and a crest and not broken either.

"By the way," Elizabeth added, "if a small parcel arrives that looks expensive and behaves itself, it is mine."

"Behaves itself?" he said.

"It doesn't explode," she translated. "It is not for you. Or it might be, but not like *that*."

"I aim for discretion but am frequently outvoted."

"Then practise," she said, and left him with the scent of winter air and a tiny ferocious hope that maybe this Christmas would not, in fact, catch fire.

Twilight arranged itself with taste. The shop windows grew brave; the bakery set out a plate marked *Spare Spatula's* that no one had the nerve to take. In the tower, the bells gave themselves a talking-to and promised to behave. The Red Lion filled with people who had not intended to stay and now could not leave without rudeness. At the post office, the last post went with a heroic wheeze.

This was the hour when St Michael's felt like a painting—the kind where nothing moves until you glance away. It was also the hour when the story reached its small crisis.

Mrs Dawson, returning to the shop to fetch her umbrella (so virtuous an errand it practically curtseyed), found on the counter a red, gold-edged envelope, the very species she had been warned about, addressed to *Canon David Thomlinson*. She did not open it, because she did not do crimes, but she did hold it up against the light, because she believed in illumination. A square shadow sat within, small as a promise.

"Gerald!" she called.

"Yes, dear?"

She put the envelope down as if it were a sleeping snake. "Nothing. Merely Providence."

She delivered it to the vicarage with the solemnity of a crown and went home feeling dangerously useful.

David, who had been considering whether the third point of his sermon might be improved by a joke about Herod and Health & Safety (it could not), found the envelope and experienced the peculiar chill of an object that had been mishandled by fate. He opened it carefully. Inside was neither card nor invitation, but a folded note and a small velvet box.

Canon. *This is clearly not meant for me, though it found me. The stationer's "moment" appears to have become a season. Please deliver it to its rightful owner before the ball. Discretion required; drama inevitable E.*

He set the note down and cracked open the box like an old secret. The cufflinks gleamed, old-gold, intertwined initials, both intimate and anonymous. D and E. He thought of every D and E in the parish and then had the good sense to stop before the alphabet dissolved into people.

He replaced the lid and set the box beside his sermon notes. *If love is messy at Christmas, it's because God trusted us with it.* He had written the line to reassure his people and now found it mildly rude that it applied to him.

Outside, the street made the sound of the first cold night: the squeak of boots, the soft chime of a bike bell, the miniature thunder of a bin lid. He went out, because sometimes a priest went out to be seen and sometimes he went out to see.

At the hall, the star had been put to bed, Mr Perkins was released from donkey-dome, Montague lectured on the dangers of unlicensed glitter. Daisy and Megan were winding fairy lights around a trestle table that had forgiven better days. "Nearly ready for the party?" David asked.

"We will be," Daisy said. "If Montague doesn't add a finale."

"There's already a finale," Megan said. "It...

"There's already a finale," Megan said. "It involves sausage rolls."

"Good," he said. "Art needs ballast." He wished them a good evening and carried on.

At the Red Lion, Tom raised a glass. *"Roof Appeal?"* he offered.

"I shouldn't," David said.

"You should," Tom corrected, pouring something modest that smelt like good behaviour. "to keep you warm."

"Thank you," David said, and sipped. The room held warmth like a story, people leaning into it without quite noticing. Arthur Preece saluted him with a paper boat. "Vicar," he said. "I'm prepared for a flood of invitations."

"Excellent," David said. "Build an ark of tact."

Back outside, the village had softened into itself. Christmas lights had the decency to be underpowered. The sky hung close like velvet. The church lamp over the porch made a stubborn halo. It was deeply ordinary and therefore holy.

At the vicarage door he paused, listening to the silence that follows a busy day, and let it sit. Then, with the cheerful resignation that passes for courage in St Michael's, he went in to write another paragraph about gentleness and to wrap something that did not require explanation.

Across the valley, Elizabeth stood at the library window with a glass of something that admitted to being wine and watched the village shine. She did not hope her children would ring. That was not the sort of hope she did. She hoped, instead, for the satisfaction of pulling off a complicated thing in a small place—and for the deeper, more dangerous satisfaction of being forgiven when she failed. Charlotte came in with a folder and a mercy.

"Progress?" Elizabeth asked.

"The florist confirms *'tasteful,'* the band confirms electricity, and Mrs Trevelyan has triumphed over the hedgehog."

"Splendid," Elizabeth said. "And the cards?"

"Mostly repatriated. There will be talk."

"There is always talk." Elizabeth sipped. "We may as well give it something to wear."

By the time the church clock chimed six (slightly off), the day had put itself away. The misdelivered cards, having done their work, lay on mantelpieces like the last words of a comic sermon. The invitations glowed beside them, innocent as sins. In kitchens across St Michael's, people made plans they would later pretend had surprised them. In the tower, a single bell tolled, once, twice, thought better of it, and tolled again, practising being right.

And that is how the wrong cards, having spread as efficiently as influenza and considerably more cheerfully, prepared the parish for a week of mayhem and a particular Christmas in which the truth, when it came, would wear tinsel like armour and pick its way between the puddles of everyone's best intentions.

## Chapter Three
## Bells and Barrels

By the third week of Advent, St Michael's jingled like a cash register that had joined the choir. Fairy lights were strung through the churchyard yews, glowing faintly against the frost, and every cottage window had adopted a candle, a paper star, or a vague sense of competition. The bell tower chimed erratically, like a joyful drunk clearing its throat.

Inside the vicarage, Canon David Thomlinson sat at his desk, trying to persuade a sermon to end politely. His draft pages were littered with crossings-out and the phrase *joy in all circumstances*, which looked more and more like a dare. From the window he could see the church roof glittering with frost and, beyond it, the faint smoke from the Hall chimneys.

He had received a note from Elizabeth that morning—delivered, of course, by Charlotte, who looked as though she would rather have faced a firing squad than another courier job. The message was brief and entirely characteristic:

*Do drop by before the ball for a restorative glass. If nothing else, you can bless the tree. E.A.*

He'd written a courteous refusal, explaining that his Advent calendar currently consisted entirely of meetings. Elizabeth would understand; she valued formality, even when she ignored it.

He rose to stretch his legs, looking around the study as if seeing it afresh: the sagging bookcases, the mismatched chairs donated by generations of parishioners, the faint smell of candle wax and hope. The radiator gurgled half-heartedly. He picked up the kettle, filled it, and paused to rub a finger across a photograph of his ordination group, young faces, bright eyes, the sort of optimism that thought theology could be tidy. The house felt larger in winter, echoing with the absences of people he had never got round to inviting. He stirred his tea, made a note to check the church heating, and wondered if loneliness counted as fasting.

Across the green, the village was in a state of festive siege. Mrs Dawson had commandeered the shop window for the choir raffle—three hampers, two bath sets, and an alarming amount of tinsel. Anwen Hughes at the bakery was baking mince pies by the regiment. Arthur Preece was lecturing anyone within earshot about the correct theological symbolism of fig pudding.

By ten o'clock gossip had travelled faster than the post. The mysterious cufflinks had re-entered circulation as legend: D and E, some said, stood for *David and Elizabeth*; others swore it meant *Divine Endurance.* Beryl Wills, who considered herself the custodian of parish truth, favoured the romantic theory. She told it to the butcher, the postman, and the milkman, each in confidence.

At the post office, Mrs Dawson leaned over the counter like a general at a war table. "Now, Bert," she said to the postmaster, "you're absolutely certain all the Ashdown Hall envelopes went out?"

"As certain as I am that you'll tell me if they didn't," said Bert, stamping parcels.

"I just hope no one mixed up the vicar's post again. You know how *delicate* some of Mrs Ashdown's correspondence can be."

"Delicate's one word," Bert said. "Explosive's another."

"Same family," said Mrs Dawson crisply. "Anyway, I'm off to supervise the raffle tickets. We can't have the choir drawing their own names again."

"Last time that was divine intervention," Bert muttered, but she was already gone, trailed by the faint scent of lavender and control.

At the Hall, Elizabeth was conducting a campaign of controlled chaos. The Christmas Ball now loomed like an exam; every detail was being rehearsed down to the scent of the candles. Charlotte shadowed her with a clipboard, ticking boxes, unticking others, and discreetly removing a taxidermy fox that had appeared under the staircase labelled *Festive Accent*.

"Charlotte," Elizabeth said, pausing mid-arrangement of lilies, "how are the bell ringers progressing with their *practice party*?"

"Mrs Wills has borrowed the hall keys, Montague has borrowed reality, and the rest are bringing casseroles."

"Excellent. One must encourage local culture."

"Even when it's loud and drunk?"

"Especially then," Elizabeth said. "Noise prevents introspection."

She moved to the window, watching the gardeners thread lights through the yews. For a moment she caught sight of the church beyond the frost-clouded lawns. It glimmered with a simplicity that irritated her. There were days when she missed her husband fiercely, and days when she merely missed being someone's certainty.

Down in the village, Mrs Dawson was holding what she called a *"raffle-strategy meeting"* with Anwen in the bakery, which meant eating a second scone and reorganising everyone else's business. "It's the bell ringers tonight," she said. "Nothing ever stays secret after the bell ringers."

"Nor should it," said Anwen. "They're better than Facebook."

"They say the vicar's name was on the cufflinks."

"They say lots of things," Anwen replied. "Usually loudly."

"Still," Mrs Dawson mused, "if there *were* a connection, it would be rather poetic, faith and society, joined in metal."

"You just like weddings," Anwen said.

"That too." Mrs Dawson bit into her scone with missionary conviction.

By early afternoon snow began to drift down in light, distracted flakes, just enough to squeak beneath boots. Canon David spent the hours visiting parishioners: the Perkins brothers, who maintained the tower clock and argued about each chime; old Mr Pettigrew, who believed Advent was invented to sell calendars; and Mrs Gibbons, who offered him fruitcake hard enough to qualify as building material. Each visit produced a small confession disguised as conversation, and by the time he reached the green again his notebook was full of errands that were really lonelinesses.

He paused outside the church. Inside, Daisy Rivers and two children were looping red ribbon along the pew ends. She looked up when the door opened. "Oh, Canon! I didn't hear you come in. Mind the paint, Montague decided the angels needed more blush."

"They look scandalised," David said.

"They were," Daisy replied, smiling. She wiped her hands. "We're decorating for the carol service. Or committing vandalism with purpose, depends who you ask."

"It's perfect," he said. "A touch of hope never hurt anyone."

She tilted her head, studying him. "You look tired."

"Occupational hazard."

"I thought joy was, too."

That earned her a quiet laugh, low and real. "You've been listening to my sermons."

"Someone has to."

They shared a smile that lingered half a second too long before she turned back to her ribbon. Outside, the bells gave a lazy clunk as if clearing their throats for evening.

Montague arrived at the hall hours before anyone else, armed with tinsel, extension cords, and artistic fervour. The result resembled an explosion in a fairy-light factory. Strands of glitter looped through the rafters; the Christmas tree leaned at an angle suggesting theological doubt. A banner painted by the schoolchildren proclaimed, in heroic capitals, **PEACE ON EARTH (SUBJECT TO AVAILABILITY).**

Beryl Wills stood in the doorway, arms folded. "It looks like Christmas threw up in here."

Her husband, David Wills, surveyed it with satisfaction. "Festive, isn't it?"

"Festive and flammable."

Montague popped up from behind the tree, dusted in glitter. "You'll thank me when the *Telegraph* sends a photographer."

"They won't," Beryl said. "They still remember the custard-cannon."

"That was art!"

"That was pudding in the font," she replied.

Preparations continued with the urgency of people who feared silence. Megan Lewis arrived balancing sausage rolls; Arthur Preece brought a trifle and an opinion about everything. Someone produced a plastic Nativity, though half the shepherds had migrated into the manger. Snow tapped gently on the windows.

By dusk, St Michael's was glowing from every window. Children dragged sledges across the green; the pub door breathed out cloves and laughter. David paused outside the bakery to buy a mince pie, declined a second on grounds of pastoral dignity, and continued up the lane, nodding to every gossip in turn.

By seven the first bell ringers assembled, armed with casseroles, bottles of sherry, and the optimism that precedes poor decisions. The urn hissed, the fairy lights flickered, and Montague, dressed in a velvet waistcoat and a sprig of mistletoe large enough to constitute flora, announced "Friends, musicians, fellow enthusiasts of campanology! Let the revels commence!"

Beryl eyed him. "Campanology sounds contagious."

"Only if done badly," he said.

David Wills clapped for order. "Right, lovelies! No climbing the tower, no ringing anything heavier than yourself, and if anyone finds last year's clapper, it is *not* to be used as a weapon."

Cheers proved that half the company hadn't listened. "To Christmas!" he cried. "May our ropes stay strong and our hangovers short!"

"Hear, hear!" Montague topped up glasses.

For a while it was almost civilised. Someone started a quiz ("Name three saints associated with bells"), someone else answered ("None, because God has mercy"), and laughter loosened into song. Beryl presided over the buffet like a queen, while Daisy circulated with plates, her cheeks glowing from kitchen heat. Outside, David Thomlinson's footsteps crunched on the path. He could hear the laughter through the door and almost went in, then thought better of it. He'd promised himself an early night and two hours of quiet. Instead, he stopped at the pub, exchanged a blessing for a glass of something hot, and listened while Tom Evans the landlord described, in thrilling detail, how the bell ringers had already shorted the lights twice.

By the time David reached the hall the sound inside had reached festival volume. Through the window he could see Montague gesturing grandly at the fairy lights and Beryl shaking her head like a long-suffering saint. Inside, the party had reached that delicate point where enthusiasm outruns wisdom. Montague unveiled his new game: *Pass the Parcel of Sin.* Each layer of wrapping contained a forfeit scribbled on paper torn from an old prayer book. By the fourth round Mrs Perkins had been forced to sing *"Silent Night"* in German. By the fifth Beryl had been crowned "Most Improper Use of Cassock."

Daisy laughed until her sides hurt. For a moment the heaviness of the past weeks—the gossip, the mistaken cards, the vicar's tired gentleness—lifted. She was still smiling when the music stopped and the parcel landed in her lap. She unwrapped a layer and found, not a scrap of paper, but a small velvet box.

"Oh!" she said. "That's not one of the prizes."

Montague leaned closer. "What have we there?"

Inside gleamed a pair of gold cufflinks, engraved with the letters *D and E*. The room leaned closer collectively.

Beryl gasped. "Those are *his!*"

"Whose?" asked half the room.

"The vicar's! D for David, E for Elizabeth!"

Montague clasped his hands. "Oh, delicious. Proof at last!"

"Proof of what?" Daisy said, more sharply than she meant.

"Proof that there's more than theology between the pulpit and the pew," Beryl said.

Laughter rippled. Daisy shut the box quickly. "They're probably just a raffle prize."

"Then why velvet?" Montague asked. "And why engraved?"

"Because some people have taste," she said. "And because the rest of you have imaginations the size of the collection plate."

That quieted them—for a while. The game resumed; the wine did not. Outside, snow swirled harder, tapping the windows like gossip itself. An hour later the urn ran dry, the sausages vanished, and the sensible people went home. The rest, led inevitably by Montague, began a spontaneous carol sing-off.

Beryl took soprano, David Wills attempted harmony, and Montague, inspired by something indefinable, began conducting with a length of bell rope. It went well until he tripped over the plug of the fairy lights and plunged the hall into darkness. A shriek, a clatter, the smell of singed paper. When the lights flickered back on, the papier mâché angel was on fire and Beryl was beating it out with a hymn book.

"Is it out?" gasped Daisy.

"It is now," Beryl said, fanning smoke. "And if that doesn't count as an exorcism, I don't know what does."

Montague, unhurt but unrepentant, poured more wine. "I'd call that a successful tableau."

"Tableau?" said David Wills. "We nearly summoned the Fire Brigade."

"Better publicity than last year," Montague replied.

The door opened then, letting in a gust of cold air and Canon David himself, wrapped in his scarf like an apology. The room fell momentarily silent, then erupted in guilty bustle: people tidying, hiding glasses, pretending sobriety.

"Evening, everyone," he said pleasantly. "I heard singing all the way from the rectory, thought I'd check the roof was still attached."

"It's... fellowship," said Beryl. "In liquid form."

"So I see."

Montague approached, flushed with both wine and mischief. "Canon, perhaps you'd do us the honour of drawing the raffle?"

David hesitated. "Is there one?"

"There is now," said Montague, brandishing a biscuit tin full of folded scraps.

"Very well." He plunged a hand in. "The winner of... whatever this is... Mrs Daisy Rivers."

Applause and wolf-whistles followed as Daisy stepped forward, cheeks glowing.

"And the prize?" asked the vicar.

Montague looked around helplessly, then seized the nearest unopened box—Daisy's handbag. "This!"

Daisy froze. "Oh no, that's..."

But he had already opened it, triumphantly revealing the cufflinks.

"Oh, how fitting!" crowed Beryl. "The vicar presents his own to his—"

"Enough," said David sharply.

The room froze. His tone wasn't angry—just firm, weary, human. "Those cufflinks belong to someone else. They were misplaced, not donated. And I suggest we all remember that Christmas is about goodwill, not speculation."

For a second, silence. Then Montague, chastened, bowed slightly. "Of course, Canon. My apologies. Artistic exuberance."

"Quite," he said dryly, taking the box back. "I'll see these returned to their owner."

He pocketed them, nodded to Daisy, who looked both mortified and oddly relieved, and departed, the cold closing behind him.

"Oops," Montague said into the hush.

Beryl poured herself another sherry. "Well," she said, "he didn't deny it."

"Didn't confirm it either," muttered David Wills. "And if we're all still alive tomorrow, that'll be a Christmas miracle."

Outside, the church clock struck nine, then ten, each chime slightly crooked as if the bells themselves were tipsy. Inside, the party rallied, fuelled by embarrassment and brandy. Someone produced a tambourine, someone else a dance step no one recognised, and by midnight the hall looked as if joy had staged a coup.

At the Hall, Elizabeth listened as Charlotte recounted the story. "Fire, scandal, and improvised raffles," she said, swirling her brandy. "I can't decide whether to send flowers or a solicitor."

"Should I deny the cufflinks were yours?" Charlotte asked carefully.

"My dear, denial is for the innocent. I prefer mystery." She smiled, faint and private. "Still, perhaps I'll visit the vicar tomorrow. Clarify our reputations before they breed."

Daisy walked home through snow that squeaked beneath her boots, the night still trembling with laughter and bells. She thought of the vicar's face when the cufflinks appeared—not anger, but a kind of sorrow. Whoever D and E really were, she sensed it wasn't what the village imagined. When she passed the church, she paused. Through the frosted window she saw him inside—alone, setting the pulpit Bible straight, adjusting candles that needed no adjusting. He looked up and caught sight of her; she half-raised a hand in greeting. He smiled, a small and genuine smile, then nodded once, as if to say *thank you,* or perhaps *patience.*

Back at the vicarage, David placed the cufflinks on his desk, beside the half-finished sermon and the mug of cold tea. The room was quiet except for the faint tick of the clock and the distant creak of the frost. He turned one cufflink over in his palm and murmured to no one in particular, "Lord, give them kindness, or failing that, short memories." Then, sighing, he went to stoke the fire.

The bells above the village gave a single accidental note, like a sigh. Daisy walked on, her breath misting before her like secrets she wasn't yet ready to tell.

## Chapter Four
## Panto, Secretly

By the third week of December, St Michael's had begun to resemble a snow globe someone had forgotten to stop shaking. Fairy lights blinked through misted windows, paper stars hung lopsided in shopfronts, and gossip travelled faster than the post. In the hall, beneath a ceiling of drafts and fairy lights, the word rehearsal was being used with reckless optimism. Montague's clandestine pantomime, THE FAIRY GODMOTHER OF BETHLEHEM, had outgrown its original purpose as a small fundraiser for the church roof and become a village-wide conspiracy. Half the parish now knew about it, which in St Michael's meant everyone except the vicar officially knew.

Mrs Dawson had appointed herself Stage Manager, Prompt and Keeper of Discipline, armed with a clipboard and the authority of someone who had once organised a parish jumble sale without casualties. Beryl Wills ran costumes with an iron thimble and a talent for constructive criticism. Daisy Rivers, against her better judgement, had agreed to play the Fairy Godmother. She suspected she had been chosen less for acting ability than because Montague thought she would look *"radiant under tinsel."*

"Projection, dear," Mrs Dawson called from the front row as Daisy attempted a line.

"There aren't any cheap seats," muttered Beryl behind the curtain. "We're not charging."

"Then reach the morally cheap ones," Mrs Dawson replied without looking up.

Snow brushed against the windows, and the air inside smelled of dust, glue and ambition. The vicarage clock struck eight somewhere beyond the frost, and Daisy wondered why she hadn't said no more firmly when she'd had the chance.

A week earlier the production had nearly died in its cradle. The first casting meeting in the church hall had collapsed over the question of Joseph. Montague wanted gravitas and cheekbones; Mr Perkins wanted immunity. After much sighing and a promise that Joseph's solo would be cut, he had consented on the condition he could wear his own sandals. The Angel Gabriel had resigned after discovering she was allergic to polyester wings, and the two shepherds had joined only when told they could keep the sheep props as compensation.

Montague, standing on a chair, had declared, "Friends, this is not mere entertainment, this is evangelism with choreography!"

Mrs Dawson, ticking names, had replied, "And without insurance."
"Art requires risk," he said grandly.

"Not the tetanus kind," she muttered.

Costumes were improvised from anything that didn't move: old curtains, choir surplices, one of Mrs Perkins's tablecloths. The donkey costume had been patched so many times it now looked more like a philosophical concept than an animal. "It'll do," said Beryl. "No one's coming for realism."

By midweek secrecy had begun to leak. At the Red Lion, the evening drinkers were already on their second round of speculation.

"I hear the vicar's in it," said Tom Evans, polishing a glass.

"He's not," said Mrs Jenkins. "He's writing the foreword."

"Someone told me Elizabeth Ashdown's sponsoring the costumes."

"She'd never. Not unless the Fairy Godmother comes with a title deed."

"Beryl says they've got a glitter cannon."

"They're in a wooden hall, Tom. Glitter and God don't mix."

Tom grinned. "Round here they're practically synonyms."

Outside, the snow fell with quiet amusement while, inside, half the village debated whether the production would be miraculous or actionable.

Back in the hall Montague clapped his hands for order. "Right, everyone! We begin at the Angelic Announcement and finish at the Happy Ending. Think pathos, think pageant, think piety with pizazz!"

Mr Perkins raised a hand. "Do I have to do the tap-dance bit?"

"Absolutely. It's post-modern."

Mrs Dawson frowned. "I don't trust anything post-modern. It sounds unlicensed."

"Art needs courage," Montague cried, gesturing to the glitter cannon borrowed from the secondary school drama department. "When the Fairy Godmother blesses the manger...*boom*...redemption in confetti form!"

Beryl folded her arms. "Last time we tried one of those it took a week to get the bits out of the font."

"That," said Montague, "was baptismal serendipity."

"Do it again," she said, "and it'll be your funeral liturgy."

Meanwhile Canon David Thomlinson was trudging through his pastoral visits, which in December meant being fed mince pies and opinions. At Raven Cottage he was told the choir needed new cassocks "preferably ones that breathe." At the Red Lion he was informed that the quiz team would dedicate their next win to "the ongoing drama at the vicarage." By the time he reached the hall the muffled sound of applause and something resembling song was drifting into the night.

He checked the parish calendar, no bookings. He knocked once and stepped inside.

Montague, in a silver cape and false eyelashes, froze mid pirouette. Daisy, haloed in fairy wings, was blessing a wooden manger while Beryl barked orders. The donkey had collapsed.
"Canon!" Montague squeaked. "You're early!"

"For what?" asked David. "The second coming?"

"A... safety inspection," Mrs Dawson said briskly, appearing at his elbow with her clipboard. "We're testing acoustics. Echo, echo, Amen."

"Indeed," said David mildly. "It sounds remarkably like a pantomime."

Montague's voice leapt an octave. "Certainly not! This is an interpretive rehearsal for... spiritual enrichment."

"Monty," said Beryl from the wings, "he's seen the fairy wings. Stop lying."

David looked around the room: the laughter, the tinsel, the unholy determination to do something good badly. He should have been cross. Instead he found himself smiling. "Very well," he said. "You may continue, on two conditions.

First, no pyrotechnics in consecrated buildings." Montague deflated. "Define pyrotechnics."

"Anything that explodes, smokes or sparkles unexpectedly."

"And the second?" asked Mrs Dawson.

"I want a ticket."

The cast cheered. "You're an angel in tweed, Canon," Montague said.

"Wrong production," he replied, leaving before anyone could cast him.

"From the angel scene!" Montague cried when the door shut. "Daisy, enter with grace. Remember, FEAR NOT, FOR EVEN GOD ENJOYS A BIT OF THEATRE!"

"Bit long, isn't it?" she murmured.

"Art requires scope!"

She swept in, wand slightly bent. "Fear not..." and tripped over the donkey's hind leg. The wand snapped in two.

Beryl sighed. "Fear not, she says."

"Prop malfunction," Montague said. "We'll call it symbolism."

"Symbolism doesn't pay for glue," Mrs Dawson shouted from the back.

They tried again; the donkey collapsed again. Laughter spread until Daisy gave up and giggled helplessly. Even Beryl cracked a smile. "If the Lord's watching," she said, "He's having a good laugh."

Later, when the rehearsal finally broke up, the cast crowded round the urn of mulled wine, steaming and exhausted.

"Do you think he'll really come?" Daisy asked quietly. "He was promised a ticket," Montague said, refilling his mug. "Front row. Redemption deserves good seating."

"He'll think we're fools," she said.

"My dear girl, we are," Montague replied. "It's the only honest profession left."

At Ashdown Hall that same evening Elizabeth was having her hair pinned for a portrait sitting when Charlotte entered, clutching a newspaper.

"They're putting on a pantomime," Charlotte said. "Apparently secretly."

Elizabeth's eyebrow lifted. "There are no secrets in a village, only delayed revelations."

"Mrs Dawson's stage-managing."

"Then it will be punctual, terrifying and entirely off-book."

"Shall I send flowers?"

"Tickets," Elizabeth said. "Two front row. I want to see who blushes first, the vicar or the fairy godmother."

Charlotte hesitated by the door. "Shall I also make a donation to the roof appeal in your name, ma'am?"
"By all means. It will look generous and confuse everyone."
"Of course."

Elizabeth turned to the mirror, adjusting an earring. "The trouble with this parish, Charlotte, is that it takes itself far too seriously. A little laughter might loosen the rafters."
Charlotte risked a smile. "Or bring them down." "Either way, it would make a change," Elizabeth replied.

In the Red Lion, the gossip had gained new legs. Tom Evans leaned against the bar polishing a glass that no longer needed polishing. "So, it's true then," he said, "there's a pantomime. Secret rehearsals. The vicar's been seen near the hall after hours."

Mrs Jenkins tapped her nose. "Not *after hours,* Tom. Just after sense. They say he's letting it happen for the sake of community spirit."

Arthur Preece shook his head. "He's too soft, that man. I told him once, kindness is all very well, but it never patched a roof."

"It patched you up after the choir social," someone muttered, and laughter rippled down the bar.

Tom poured another round. "Well, whatever it is, they'll have a full house. People round here love nothing better than religion with refreshments."

Outside, the snow deepened. The churchyard looked ethereal, gravestones dusted with icing sugar, the tower light blinking faintly through the flurries. From the hall came a rumble of laughter, the sound of chairs scraping, the thump of Beryl's voice declaring, "That's *not* how you hold a halo!"

Inside, the final rehearsal staggered towards chaos. Daisy's wings had lost most of their feathers, the donkey's back legs had gone missing again, and Montague was directing from a chair because he'd twisted his ankle *"in pursuit of art."*

"Everyone take five!" Mrs Dawson shouted, clapping her hands. "And for heaven's sake, no one touch the glitter cannon."

"You said that last week," muttered Beryl, tightening a hem.

"And yet here we are," Mrs Dawson replied.

Daisy sat on the edge of the stage, rubbing her ankle and staring at the flickering fairy lights. Her wand, patched and slightly singed, leaned against her knee.

"You all right, love?" Beryl asked, sitting beside her.
"Just tired," Daisy said. "It's all a bit much. People keep staring at me in church since those cufflinks appeared."
Beryl sniffed. "They'll find something else soon enough. The village attention span's shorter than a hymn intro."
"Do you think he believes the rumours?"

"The vicar? He's too clever. But clever men still feel things, you know. Don't let his sermons fool you."

Daisy smiled faintly. "He makes everything sound lighter than it is."

"That's his job, dear. You make the world lighter for everyone else; someone's got to do it for him."
Montague clapped again. "Back to places! This time with conviction. Remember, we're saving souls and selling tickets!" Beryl muttered, "More like the other way round."

The run-through began anew. Daisy swept onto the stage, wand raised, voice strong now. "Fear not, for even God enjoys a bit of theatre!" The line drew applause from the back, even from Mrs Dawson, who pretended she was only swatting dust. The angel choir came in three beats late. Joseph forgot his cue. The donkey, miraculously, remained upright. Montague declared it divine intervention.

When the rehearsal finally ended near midnight, the cast tumbled out into the snowy dark, laughing, coughing, glowing with the sort of exhausted pride only small triumphs bring. Daisy lingered to lock up the hall, brushing stray glitter from her coat. Across the green, the vicarage windows were still lit. She hesitated, half tempted to knock and return the borrowed hymn books stacked in her bag. Instead, she watched her breath bloom white in the air, then turned for home.

Canon David was indeed awake. The sermon he'd been shaping all week sat half-finished on his desk, paragraphs abandoned mid-thought. His mind, traitorously, kept returning to the sight of fairy wings in lamplight and the laughter that had filled the hall. He'd gone to bed once already and risen again, restless. Now he stood at the window with a mug of tea gone cold, watching the snow fall in perfect indifference. The cufflinks lay on the desk beside the open Bible, gleaming faintly. He still hadn't found their rightful owner, though the gossip pages of the parish seemed determined to assign them meaning.

He picked one up, turned it over between his fingers, and murmured, "D and E... devotion and embarrassment, most likely." Then he smiled at the absurdity of talking to jewellery and set it down again.

He returned to his sermon, crossing out whole lines, adding others. *Truth, even when wrapped in folly, still shines.* Then, after a moment's thought, *Sometimes folly is the only wrapping people will open.*

The house creaked in the cold. He heard the wind fussing at the chimney, the faint echo of laughter still drifting from the hall. He envied them a little, their certainty that joy could be made simply by trying. He remembered what Elizabeth had once said to him in a quieter season: "Churches fall down because people forget to play." Perhaps she was right.

He sat again, dipping his pen. Beneath the sermon draft he added one more line: *If faith is to survive, it must learn to dance, even badly.*

At Ashdown Hall, Elizabeth was still awake too, sitting at her dressing table with a brandy in hand and the faint smile of a woman who both admires and pities the village she rules. Charlotte entered softly, carrying a folded note.

"From Mrs Dawson, ma'am. Confirmation of your two tickets. She says they're front row."

Elizabeth nodded, amused. "I do like a ringside seat at human nature. Have the car ready early that evening. We'll make a spectacle of punctuality."
"Yes, ma'am."

Elizabeth turned back to the window. Snow fell thick across the lawns, softening the edges of everything. "You know, Charlotte, I think I almost miss being surprised. Perhaps the pantomime will manage it."

Charlotte smiled. "It usually does, one way or another."
Across the green, lights in the hall winked out one by one. The frost settled, the bells gave a lazy, uneven chime. In the quiet vicarage, David finally closed his notebook, set the cufflinks gently aside, and whispered a small, private prayer: "Lord, bless their madness. And if You can't, at least make it harmless." Then he drew the curtains, banked the fire, and let the night have the last word.

Outside, the snow thickened until even the church tower looked hushed. Somewhere, under all that stillness, the laughter of the rehearsal lingered, bright as a candle left burning in an empty nave. The village slept, dreaming of costumes, glitter, and grace, while the bells, crooked, faithful, slightly tipsy, counted down the days until Christmas.

## Chapter Five
## Mistletoe Mechanics

The day of the Ashdown Christmas Ball dawned too bright to trust. The sky was a bleached winter blue that promised snow later, and the frost along the hedgerows glittered as if it had ideas above its station. From the church tower one could see the long drive of Ashdown Hall sweeping up the hill, already being cleared of snow by two men in flat caps who were loudly arguing about whether they were underpaid or under-appreciated.

In the village, the excitement was electric. The butcher was slicing ham "for sandwiches, not gossip," the florist had sold out of holly, and the postmaster had pinned a handwritten notice to the window reading: NO, I CAN'T GET YOU ON THE GUEST LIST.

Inside the Hall, the preparations had started before dawn. Footmen wrestled with garlands that refused to hang symmetrically, and Charlotte prowled the corridors with her clipboard like a benevolent warden. Every few minutes she ticked something, unticked something else, and reminded herself to breathe.

Elizabeth Ashdown appeared at ten o'clock precisely, gliding down the staircase in a dressing gown that cost more than most people's cars. "Charlotte, darling, have we located the silver napkin rings with the crest?"

"Yes, ma'am. They were in the billiard room cupboard with the spare candelabra."

"Excellent. I'd hate for the clergy to think we'd gone minimalist."

By mid-afternoon the Hall was a symphony of noise: florists, caterers, and musicians all tuning, polishing, and colliding. The scent of pine and beeswax filled the air. Outside, the snow had started again, thin flakes drifting lazily across the parkland as if testing the atmosphere for gossip.

In the village shop, Mrs Dawson was supervising a covert meeting disguised as a bread queue. "You must understand," she was saying to Beryl Wills, "that an Ashdown Ball is not simply a party. It's a moral test."

Beryl examined a jar of mincemeat. "You've failed already."

"On the contrary," Mrs Dawson said. "I'm attending as a representative of the parish. Someone must maintain standards."

"While wearing sequins," Beryl muttered.

Daisy arrived breathless, clutching a borrowed evening bag. "Has anyone seen my invitation? I think it blew out of the window."

Mrs Dawson looked horrified. "One does not LOSE an Ashdown invitation. It's practically a sacrament." "I'm sure they'll still let me in," Daisy said hopefully.

"Perhaps," Beryl said. "If you arrive with a casserole."

At the vicarage, Canon David Thomlinson stood in front of his mirror attempting to persuade a bowtie to behave. The tie, being silk and opinionated, refused. He muttered a short, undignified prayer and tried again. Finally he surrendered and left it slightly crooked. There was, he decided, a certain honesty in imperfection.

The study behind him was scattered with sermon drafts, each sheet carrying the ghosts of Advent thoughts that hadn't quite found their endings. He'd promised himself an early night; instead he was about to walk into a ballroom full of speculation. He smiled ruefully. "Onward, then," he told the mirror, "unto glamour and probable humiliation."

By seven o'clock, cars and taxis were crunching up the drive. The Hall glowed like a lantern on the hill, its windows spilling gold across the snow. The air smelled of pine, smoke and expensive anticipation. The invitation had promised CAROLS, CHAMPAGNE, AND CHARITY RAFFLE, BLACK TIE, GOOD SENSE OPTIONAL. The village, of course, had taken the optional part to heart.

Inside, the marble hall shimmered with candlelight. Guests surrendered coats and composure to the footmen. Laughter ricocheted off the high ceilings; sequins and ambition mingled freely. At the top of the staircase stood Elizabeth herself, queen, hostess, ringmaster — greeting each guest with warmth precisely calibrated to their usefulness.

"Mr and Mrs Barlow, how divine. You've come dressed as prosperity itself."

"Montague, still velvet? I see subtlety continues to elude you."

"Mrs Dawson, so brave of you to leave the parish unsupervised."

She smiled and glittered and managed the impossible: to make every person feel both seen and slightly judged.

Charlotte hovered at her shoulder with the guest list. "If anyone asks about the seating," she murmured, "tell them it's alphabetical by moral worth."

"Too late," Elizabeth whispered back. "I've already seated Mrs Dawson opposite Montague for balance."

Canon David arrived fashionably late, which in clerical terms meant twenty minutes behind his conscience. His dinner jacket was ten years old, his shoes polished to within an inch of confession, and he'd already promised himself not to mention the roof fund before dessert.

"Canon!" Elizabeth glided towards him, radiant in emerald silk and diamonds that probably had names. "You've come. How very obedient."

"I do try to follow divine instruction," he said, smiling. "Yours, in this case."

"Flattery from a clergyman. How refreshing. Come, rescue me from Montague; he's been explaining post-modern theology to the wine waiter."

Montague turned, already glowing like a festive beetroot. "Canon! You look positively rakish. Tell me, is your sermon nearly written, or shall we add you to the pantomime cast?" "Only if you require someone to multiply loaves and fishes," said David. "Or confiscate your glitter."

Beryl Wills appeared beside the canapé table, glass already in hand. "Evening, Canon. We've had a sweepstake, how long before Mrs Dawson mentions the rumour?"

"Has she already?"

"Twice," Beryl said. "And it's only seven-thirty."

Across the room Mrs Dawson had cornered Charlotte by the buffet. "My dear, you must admit it's suspicious. Invitations, cufflinks, dinners at the Hall — one doesn't misdeliver that sort of intimacy by accident."

Charlotte, who had reached the end of her patience, replied, "Mrs Dawson, if gossip were an Olympic sport, you'd be wearing gold by now."

Mrs Dawson sniffed. "I'm merely observant."

"You're an entire surveillance department."

Before she could reply, the orchestra struck up a waltz. Elizabeth clapped her hands lightly. "Ladies and gentlemen, let us begin, and remember, dance as if you believe the world is watching. Because in this village, it is."

The dance floor filled with the rustle of silk and the shuffle of nerves. David found himself partnered with Daisy who looked disconcertingly elegant in blue satin. Her usual brightness was tempered with something quieter, almost careful.

"You don't dance like a vicar," she said.

"I've been tutored by parish fetes and fear."

She laughed, relaxing. "I'm glad you're here. Everyone's been talking."

"Ah," he said. "Then the village is still functioning."

"It's not fair, though, the gossip."

"When was St Michael's ever fair?"

She hesitated, then said, "You're too kind to her."

"To Elizabeth?" "She plays with people," Daisy said softly. "Beautifully, but still..."

He looked down at her. "Sometimes people perform because truth is harder to bear."

The music swelled. Around them sequins shimmered, champagne corks popped, and laughter rose like incense. Montague swept past in a cloud of velvet and aftershave, leading a bewildered Mrs Perkins through a turn that nearly uprooted a floral display. Beryl and her husband moved with surprising grace, although she managed to whisper commentary throughout.

As the waltz ended, applause rippled. Elizabeth, watching from the top of the stairs, caught David's eye. There was humour there, and something just on the edge of challenge.

The evening unfolded like clockwork dressed in silk. Waiters circulated with champagne; the string quartet slid from Handel into Gershwin with genteel rebellion. A footman refilled glasses with the solemnity of communion.

In one corner, Montague had trapped two councillors in a lecture about THEOLOGY AND TAP,DANCE: A MANIFESTO. In another, Mrs Dawson had stationed herself strategically near the mistletoe, ostensibly to ensure no impropriety while clearly hoping for some.

It was then that the first commotion began, a low murmur near the dessert table that grew into laughter. Someone had hung a spectacular sprig of mistletoe directly above the raffle prizes (later blamed on Montague). Combined with champagne and reckless goodwill, it produced what the parish magazine would later call *"unseemly seasonal enthusiasm."*

Beryl was caught under it twice, once with her husband and once, to general delight, with Mrs Dawson, "An administrative error," she claimed afterwards. Montague attempted to kiss his own reflection in the punch bowl and succeeded in baptising his sleeve.

Elizabeth floated serenely through the chaos, collecting anecdotes as other people collected drinks. She paused by the grand piano, where Daisy was now sitting, pretending to study the sheet music. "My dear, you look enchanting," Elizabeth said. "Blue suits you. It suggests sincerity, such a rare quality at parties."

"Thank you," Daisy said. "You look... magnificent."

Elizabeth smiled, gracious and dangerous. "Magnificence is simply sincerity with better tailoring." She drifted away before Daisy could answer.

David, meanwhile, was trying to extricate himself from a conversation with the mayor about car park theology when someone tugged his sleeve. He turned — and found himself face to face with Elizabeth beneath the mistletoe.

"Well," she said lightly, eyes gleaming. "What would the vicarage say?"

"They'd probably issue a press release," he murmured.

"Then we'd better disappoint them."

She moved aside before anyone could exhale, leaving only laughter and speculation in her wake. The whole exchange lasted seconds but would occupy parish imagination for months. Mrs Dawson saw it, of course; she saw everything. Within an hour she'd mentally drafted three versions of the story, each more dramatic than the last.

At half-past nine Elizabeth took the stage for the raffle draw, graceful as a queen addressing her court. "Ladies and gentlemen," she began, "thank you for your generosity. Tonight's proceeds will ensure the church roof remains above reproach, unlike most of us." Laughter rolled through the room. "Canon, would you do the honours?"

David stepped forward, resigned and amused. The first prize, a luxury hamper, went to Mr Perkins. The second, dinner for two at the Red Lion, to Daisy, who blushed crimson. The third, a mystery box, was handed to Mrs Dawson.

Elizabeth leaned down, smiling like a benevolent executioner. "My dear, may it bring you all the surprise you've brought the rest of us."

Mrs Dawson opened it, and froze. Inside lay a small velvet box. Gasps rippled. Elizabeth blinked. "Oh, for heaven's sake. Not again."

David took it gently from her hand. "These," he said clearly, "belong to no one in this room."

"Except perhaps you, Canon," Montague called, too pleased with himself.

"Perhaps," David said, "but not tonight." He slipped the box into his pocket. "Now, if you'll excuse me, I have a sermon to finish, before someone turns it into musical theatre."

Laughter broke the tension. Elizabeth caught his eye as he stepped down. There was gratitude there, and something else she wasn't ready to name.

The ballroom began to exhale once the raffle was done. The orchestra slipped into something softer, a tune that sounded like champagne remembering its bubbles. Waiters cleared glasses, guests relaxed into gossip, and the grand chandelier shimmered as though eavesdropping.

Elizabeth resumed her role as generalissimo of charm, moving through her guests with the skill of someone simultaneously performing and evaluating. To the untrained eye, she was simply radiant. To Charlotte, hovering dutifully with a clipboard disguised as a fan, she looked like a woman holding a dozen threads and hoping none would snap.

In a far corner, Montague had commandeered the pianist. "Something with gusto!" he demanded, before breaking into a rendition of *Good King Wenceslas* that would have alarmed livestock. People applauded politely; some fled. Mrs Dawson whispered, "Artistic enthusiasm," which in her mouth was a diagnosis.

Daisy lingered near the window, the cold seeping gently through the glass. The lights of the village flickered faintly below, and for a moment she longed for the simplicity of the church hall with its uneven chairs and honest draughts. Here, every smile was lacquered, every laugh curated. Yet she couldn't entirely resist the enchantment of it — the music, the laughter, the way the snow outside caught the light like grace in disguise.

"Escaping?" The voice came quietly. David stood beside her, a glass of something sparkling in hand.

"Just admiring the view," she said.
"Beautiful, isn't it?"

"Yes," she replied, "but it doesn't feel real."

He looked out at the snow. "Reality tends to be less symmetrical."

They stood in companionable silence for a moment. The faint scent of pine and perfume drifted between them. "You handled the raffle well," she said softly.

"Practice," he answered. "Parish life is mostly incident management."

"And cufflink retrieval."

"That too."

She glanced up at him. "Are they really yours?"
He hesitated. "No," he said finally. "And yet somehow, I suspect they belong to me all the same."

Across the room, Elizabeth was laughing at something Montague had said, but her eyes, as if by instinct, flicked toward them. The sight of David and Daisy in quiet conversation made something twist in her chest, an emotion she couldn't decide was envy, fondness, or warning.

Charlotte approached then, murmuring, "All's well, ma'am. The kitchen has survived and the guests seem content."

"Of course they are," said Elizabeth, her tone lightly ironic. "I've bribed them with alcohol and lighting." She turned back toward the dance floor. "Still, one must play the part given. The show must go on."

By eleven the hall had begun to loosen its grandeur. Shoes were abandoned discreetly under chairs, and someone had persuaded the string quartet to attempt *White Christmas*. Montague, now in possession of a tambourine, was adding percussion of uncertain rhythm.

"Charlotte," Elizabeth said, taking a last sip of champagne, "if I ever suggest combining the roof appeal with dancing again, remind me that charity is best expressed through cheques, not chassé."

"Yes, ma'am," said Charlotte dutifully, though she was smiling.

Near the hearth, Mrs Dawson was recounting the cufflink saga for the third time, embellishing freely. "And then, my dears, he said, 'these belong to no one in this room,' which is precisely what a guilty man would say.

Beryl snorted. "Or a clever one."
"Oh, he's clever," Mrs Dawson said darkly. "All the clever ones are."

Arthur Preece leaned in. "You do realise you're talking about a vicar, not a spy?"

Mrs Dawson gave him a look of such withering authority that he retreated toward the trifle.

By midnight, the orchestra was beginning to pack up, and guests, sensing the spell thinning, started their goodbyes. The great doors opened to reveal a night newly dusted with snow, soft flakes tumbling lazily through the lamplight. One by one the cars rolled away, leaving tracks like calligraphy on the drive.

David stood near the entrance, coat in hand, exchanging polite farewells. Elizabeth joined him, her diamonds catching the last glimmer of chandelier light.

"So, Canon," she said, "was it a success?"

"You raised enough for the roof," he said. "And probably for several future sermons."

She smiled faintly. "Do I scandalise you?"
"You keep me employed."

"That's a very Anglican answer."

"It's a very Anglican parish," he said.

For a moment they simply looked at each other — the air between them bright and fragile as frost. Then Charlotte appeared with Elizabeth's cloak, breaking the spell.
"Good night, Canon," Elizabeth said softly.

"Good night, Elizabeth."
He turned toward the door, the night greeting him like a cold baptism. Daisy was already outside, her shawl drawn tight, waiting for a taxi that refused to appear.

"Do you need a lift?" he asked.

"I can walk," she said, though her teeth betrayed her with a small chatter.

"I insist," he said gently. They walked together down the drive, the crunch of snow loud in the hush.

For a while they said nothing. Then Daisy asked, "Do you ever wish you could leave? The parish, the rumours, all of it?"

"Sometimes," he said. "But I think holiness is less about escaping and more about staying put — even when it's uncomfortable."

She smiled, looking at the glowing church below. "That sounds like you."

"And you?"

"I don't know yet," she said. "Maybe I'm still finding out."
At the foot of the hill they parted, each with the faint sense that they'd said something important without quite knowing what it was.

Back in the Hall, silence had settled like dust after applause. The staff moved quietly through the rooms, extinguishing candles, gathering glasses. Elizabeth remained alone at the tall window, gazing out toward the dark line of the church.

Charlotte returned softly. "You all right, ma'am?"

Elizabeth nodded. "Perfectly." She paused. "Tell me, Charlotte, do you ever tire of other people's stories?"

"Constantly," Charlotte said.

"And yet we can't stop listening."

"No, ma'am."

Elizabeth smiled faintly. "Nor creating them, it seems."

Charlotte hesitated. "Do you think they'll stop talking?"

"Oh, never," said Elizabeth. "But gossip, like faith, needs fresh miracles." She turned back to the window, her reflection mingling with the snow beyond. "Let them talk. It means they're still looking."

Outside, the bells of St Michael's struck midnight, slightly off-time, as always, their sound rolling across the valley like laughter that refused to die.

In the vicarage below, David removed his bowtie, hung up his coat, and sat by the fire. He took the small velvet box from his pocket, opened it, and studied the initials gleaming in the firelight. D and E. He sighed, then smiled, not in resignation, but in understanding.

On the desk nearby, his unfinished sermon waited. He dipped his pen, wrote one final line, and read it aloud softly:

*"Grace, after all, is simply love behaving itself under observation."*

The fire crackled, the bells faded, and the snow kept falling, gentle and endless, upon a village that mistook mischief for mystery and found God somewhere in between.

## Chapter Six
## Midnight Misfires

Christmas Eve crept into St Michael's beneath a sky like frozen glass. The village woke to frost on every hedge, smoke curling from every chimney, and the faint, promising smell of panic. Canon David Thomlinson had been awake since half-past six. By nine he had mislaid his sermon twice, located it once, and then lost it again beneath a sheaf of choir rosters. The kettle hissed like judgement in the background. From the lane outside came the thud of boots on ice and the distant cry of Mrs Dawson informing the postman that she KNEW about the mistletoe incident and that the Bishop "would be hearing about it in due course."

He rubbed his eyes and tried to concentrate. On the desk lay his sermon draft, covered in crossings out and glitter, actual glitter, from last night's pantomime debacle. The words PEACE ON EARTH were underlined twice and now looked faintly sarcastic.

By ten o'clock the first knock came. Daisy appeared in the doorway, cheeks pink from the cold, carrying a tray of sausage rolls. "For the choir," she said.

"For bribery, you mean."

She smiled. "Same thing in December."

"True." He hesitated. "How are the wings?"

"Singed but salvageable. Mrs Dawson says I'm an emblem of resilience."

"She says that about the church boiler as well."

When she'd gone, he looked out through the frosted window. The churchyard was already busy: Beryl Wills supervising bell ringers, Montague was loading something large and suspicious into a handcart, and the verger attempting to convince a donkey that it was not required at the midnight service.

At the Red Lion the annual bell ringers' breakfast was in noisy session. The fire blazed, the floor glittered with spilt sugar, and David Wills, their captain, stood at the bar declaiming like Nelson before battle. "Right, lovelies! Tonight's the big one. Carols, bells, glory!"

Beryl, arms folded, replied, "And liver failure."

"The key," he announced, "is moderation."

"Define moderation," muttered Montague, who had wandered in to *"borrow inspiration."*

"Stopping before you regret it."

"Then we're doomed," said Montague cheerfully.

Arthur Preece from the choir entered carrying a hymnbook and the expression of a man already regretting his life choices. "Has anyone actually seen the vicar this morning?" "He's writing," said Beryl.

"Good," Arthur said. "Maybe he'll include a prayer for the bell tower. It's still sulking after Thursday's rehearsal."

The landlord brought over a tray of mince pies and a jug of something that looked seasonal and smelt dangerous. "You ringing before or after the service?"

"Before," said David Wills. "Then we can enjoy the sermon without the shakes."

"Or with them," said Beryl. "Depends who's preaching."

Montague raised his mug in salute. "To courage, to chaos, and to the enduring miracle that none of us have been excommunicated."

"Hear, hear," chorused the rest.

Across the village the pantomime troupe had re-assembled in the hall, determined to produce something resembling theatre. Mrs Dawson directed from the front with her clipboard of power; Daisy fluttered miserably behind the curtain, and Montague attempted to look visionary.

"Places!" cried Mrs Dawson. "Where's the glitter cannon?"

"Decommissioned," said Montague.

"Why?"
"The vicar forbade explosions."

"He's not here."

Montague brightened. "Then perhaps the Holy Spirit will look the other way."

Beryl entered mid-sentence, wrapped in her bell ringer's scarf. "You're STILL rehearsing? The service starts in an hour!"

"We're polishing," said Montague.

"You're smouldering," said Beryl. "The hall smells like treacle and hubris."

"Art," he replied loftily, "requires risk."

"Art," Beryl said, "requires insurance."

Onstage, Daisy attempted her opening line: "Fear not, for I bring you...oh, drat." Her halo slipped forward like a guilty thought. The shepherd tripped over the manger. The angel fell off his stool. The donkey, played by Mr Perkins in a brown cardigan, refused to move.

Mrs Dawson clapped her hands. "Splendid energy! Now again, but this time without tragedy."

At Ashdown Hall, Christmas Eve was unfolding with the poise of a military campaign. The house smelled of polish and oranges; the drawing room glowed with firelight and resentment. "Charlotte," said Elizabeth Ashdown, inspecting the table, "does it look serene?"

"Visually, yes. Emotionally, it's panicking."

"Perfect." Elizabeth adjusted a candlestick by half an inch. "Serenity is always best staged."

By the time Canon David arrived, snow had begun again, fine as flour. Charlotte showed him in with the air of a butler halfway through a nervous breakdown. "My apologies," he said, dusting snow from his coat. "I was delayed by a theological dispute in the porch." "Between whom?" asked Elizabeth.

"The choir and a robin. The robin won."

She smiled. "Do come in. You look like a Christmas card from the Temperance Society."

They sat to supper, roast capon, red wine, and the low murmur of the wireless quartet. For a while they spoke easily: parish news, the roof fund, how the village seemed simultaneously exhausted and indestructible. "Are you prepared for tonight?" she asked.

"As much as one can be. The sermon's finished, the organist isn't, and I've accepted that something will catch fire."

"How very Anglican," she said with approval.

There was a comfortable pause, the kind that only occurs between two people used to being observed. "I hear," she added lightly, "that the pantomime is already a legend." "Legends are rarely accurate," he said. "But in this case, possibly generous."

They had just begun the second course when a frantic banging came from the front. Charlotte opened it to reveal Montague, snow-spattered and incandescent with glitter. "Mrs Ashdown! Canon! Catastrophe!"

Elizabeth regarded him over her glass. "You're sparkling. Should I be concerned?"

"The pantomime!" he gasped. "It's… revolted! We've lost control of Act Two!"

"Did you ever have control?" asked David.

"The cannon misfired, Mrs Dawson's wig is aflame, the donkey's on the roof, and the bell ringers have kidnapped the wise men!"

Elizabeth set down her fork with queenly calm. "Well," she said, "that sentence has brightened my evening."

"Please," begged Montague. "You must come! You're both on the committee!"

"I'm not," said David.

"You are now!"

Elizabeth sighed, rising. "Charlotte, fetch my coat. Canon, consider this your penance."

They reached the hall to find it glowing faintly pink and smelling of caramel. Smoke coiled lazily toward the rafters. People dashed to and fro carrying buckets and excuses. Mrs Dawson, singed but unbowed, was stamping out the remnants of her script. "The cannon exploded, the donkey panicked, the fairy improvised!"

Daisy, missing one wing, waved weakly. "We brought Act Three forward."

"Which is?"

"The Nativity," she said. "With tap-dance."

Elizabeth groaned. "Dear God."

"Already invoked," said David.

Beryl burst in dragging a rope. "The bells are jammed! The clapper's stuck, and David Wills is threatening to ring it manually."

"You can't ring a bell manually!" Montague cried.

"He's trying. With a broom handle."

A crash shook the rafters. Dust rained down. "That," said David, "was either divine intervention or a health hazard." Then, inevitably, the fire alarm began.

Lights flashed, chaos bloomed anew. Half the cast bolted into the snow, including the donkey, which turned out indeed to be Mr Perkins. Montague seized a bucket; David waved his sermon at the detector. Charlotte arrived wielding a fire blanket like Joan of Arc. Within minutes the alarm died, leaving panting silence broken only by one distant, deranged bell.

Elizabeth surveyed the ruin. "Well," she said, "if this doesn't bring the parish together, nothing will."

"Except prosecution," murmured Beryl.

Steam rose from the extinguished glitter cannon. Stray flecks of silver drifted through the air like the ghosts of bad ideas. The cast stood in various stages of shock, looking as though Christmas itself had exploded over them.

Mrs Dawson adjusted what remained of her wig and announced, "That concludes the dress rehearsal." "There was nothing dressed about it," muttered Beryl.

Montague, soot-faced but unrepentant, clasped his hands. "Magnificent energy! Transcendently avant-garde! When chaos itself performs, who needs choreography?" Elizabeth folded her arms. "Montague, dear, if you ever again combine theology and pyrotechnics, I shall see to it that your name is removed from every parish rota between here and Townsend."

He bowed. "Understood, Your Grace of Glitter."

David leaned wearily against a trestle table. "Is anyone injured?"

"Only reputationally," said Beryl.

"Good. Let's keep it that way."

"Canon," Mrs Dawson said briskly, "since you're here, perhaps you could bless the hall. It's been through trauma."

He gave her a look. "The insurance company will do that on Tuesday."

The donkey costume lay in a heap by the door, steaming faintly. Daisy crouched beside it, trying to coax Mr Perkins out of the headpiece. "It's stuck," she whispered.

"Pull harder," said Beryl.

"I'm afraid I'll decapitate him."

"He's fine," said Beryl. "He's from Crawshaw. They breed sturdy."

Charlotte appeared carrying a tray of tea, which seemed both ludicrous and entirely right. "Mrs Ashdown thought everyone might need reviving."

"She was correct," said David, accepting a cup. "Though next time, perhaps something stronger."

"I can find brandy," said Charlotte.

"Leave it," said Elizabeth. "They'll only start singing again."

Outside, a wind had risen, scouring the snow from the roofs. The church bell gave an occasional uncertain clang, as if checking its lines. Somewhere beyond, the Red Lion door opened and closed; laughter carried faintly through the cold.

"Right," said Mrs Dawson. "If we're to make the midnight service, we'll need to tidy up and pretend none of this happened."

"That's the Anglican way," said Elizabeth.

"Exactly," said Mrs Dawson, missing the irony.

They set to work. Chairs were straightened, glitter swept, scripts rescued from puddles. Daisy, cheeks flushed, tried to mend her wing with tape; David helped her, holding the broken wire steady. "You've had quite a week," he said gently.

"So have you."

He smiled. "True. But you wear calamity better than I do."

She laughed, the sound tired and bright. "It's the glitter. It hides the smoke damage."

Elizabeth, watching them, felt an unexpected twinge of something she refused to name. She turned away and began stacking hymnbooks instead.

By eleven the hall was once more orderly, in the superficial sense that defined St Michael's. The pantomime had been declared a success *"in spirit if not execution."* Montague insisted on bringing the donkey head to the church "for continuity." Beryl vetoed this with the efficiency of a guillotine.

As they trudged through the snow toward the church, breath misting in the air, there was a strange camaraderie among them, the peculiar joy found only in shared disaster. The church was already glowing when they arrived, candles in every window, evergreen garlands along the pews. The air inside was fragrant with wax, pine, and the faint singed aroma of the verger's cassock.

The choir assembled like survivors. Mrs Dawson took her place at the lectern; Beryl marshalled the bell ringers with military efficiency. Montague slipped discreetly to the organ and began a cautious prelude in C major. It was, miraculously, the right key. Canon David moved slowly down the aisle, taking it all in—the candles, the carols, the exhaustion, the imperfect holiness of it all. He reached the pulpit just as the clock began to chime midnight.

He spoke quietly, at first. "It's been said that peace on earth comes gently. I think we've proved tonight that's not always true." Laughter, subdued but genuine, rippled through the pews. "Sometimes peace arrives through noise, and folly, and the stubborn joy of people who won't give up even when their glitter cannon explodes." He glanced toward Elizabeth, seated, serene, faintly smiling, and then toward Daisy, who sat among the choir, halo crooked but shining all the same. "The angels didn't sing to the perfect, or the prepared. They sang to the weary, the foolish, the cold shepherds who were simply still awake. Maybe that's our task tonight—not to shine flawlessly, but just to stay awake long enough to notice love happening, even in the chaos."

A hush fell. Outside, the wind eased. Inside, the warmth deepened. When the choir began O COME, ALL YE FAITHFUL, the sound filled the rafters like light. Beryl's descant soared; Montague's organ held its nerve. Mrs Dawson wept discreetly into her programme. By the time the candles were extinguished, it was Christmas.

The congregation drifted out into the snow, murmuring good wishes. The sky was low and luminous; the stars hung like frost caught mid-fall. Elizabeth stood by the gate, her breath silver in the air. "Well," she said as David approached, "you made theologians of us all."

"I was aiming for survival," he replied.

She smiled. "You underestimate yourself."

Charlotte joined them, pulling her coat tight. "Mrs Ashdown, the car is ready."

"In a moment," Elizabeth said. She turned back to David. "Canon, thank you, for rescuing

"Both the pantomime and the parish."

"Strictly speaking, I only slowed their collapse."

"That counts as salvation around here."

They stood for a moment in the muffled stillness. Somewhere in the distance, a single bell tolled—almost in tune.

"Good night," she said finally.

"Good morning," he corrected gently.

She hesitated, then reached up and brushed a speck of glitter from his sleeve. "You'll never be rid of it, you know."

"I've accepted that," he said. "It's baptism by panto."

She laughed softly, then turned and walked toward the waiting car.

Back at the vicarage, long after the others had gone, David sat by the fire rewriting his sermon from memory. The room smelled of wax and wood smoke; a stray scrap of tinsel glinted on the mantel like an afterthought. He wrote: PEACE ON EARTH RARELY ARRIVES QUIETLY. IT OFTEN ENTERS DISGUISED AS LAUGHTER, STUBBORNNESS, OR GLITTER—BUT IT COMES ALL THE SAME.

He paused, smiled, and underlined GLITTER. A gentle knock came at the door. He opened it to find Daisy, wrapped in a scarf too big for her, holding a small box. "I think these belong to you," she said. "They were in the props crate."

He took it, smiling. "The cufflinks again?"

"They follow you like bad theology."

"Or good grace," he said.

"Merry Christmas, Canon."

"And to you, Daisy."

When she'd gone, he sat again by the fire, opened the box, and let the gold catch the light. D and E. The letters glowed softly, their meaning no clearer but somehow kinder. He closed the lid, leaned back, and listened. Outside, the bells of St Michael's rang a little off-beat—imperfect, human, alive.

He whispered, half to himself, half to the night, "Well, Lord... at least they're ringing." And in the hush that followed, the sound seemed to answer, a clumsy, joyful, unmistakable Amen.

## Chapter Seven
## Christmas Morning

The morning arrived softly over St Michael's, pale light sliding across the snow like a benediction. The storm had passed in the night, leaving the village dusted and shimmering as if the world had finally agreed to behave itself. The church roof gleamed under the early sun, and every cottage window glowed with the first stirrings of life. It was the kind of Christmas morning that made even the cynics pause.

Inside St Michael's, hundreds of candles trembled in their holders, a gentle sea of light against the grey stone walls. The scent of pine, polish, and faint smoke drifted through the nave, part holy, part human. Every pew was filled. Coats steamed faintly, hymnbooks rustled, and the organ muttered to itself in anticipation.

In the vestry, Canon David Thomlinson was adjusting his stole in the mirror and wondering whether he was about to lead worship or supervise a sequel to last night's pantomime. The answer, he suspected, was both. Gerald Davies, the choirmaster, appeared with a sheaf of music under one arm and mild panic under the other.

"Choir ready?" David asked.

"As they'll ever be," Gerald replied. "Mrs Dawson's rewritten the descant again."

"Why?"

"She said the angels demanded more ambition."

David smiled faintly. "Of course they did." He brushed a speck of glitter, from the hem of his stole. "And Montague?"

"Claiming divine inspiration. Or indigestion. Hard to tell."

David nodded. "Then it's definitely Christmas."

They stepped into the chancel as the organ swelled. The choir began *O Come, All Ye Faithful* with a determination that could have raised the dead. The bell ringers, still traumatised from their earlier escapades, were confined to the tower under strict orders not to "experiment." Down below, the congregation shifted and whispered, exchanging news, glances, and judgements.

Mrs Dawson supervised the seating like a border official, ushering latecomers into moral compliance. The front pew was occupied by the children of the Sunday Club, half asleep and sticky with mince pies. Near the back, Montague had taken it upon himself to direct proceedings from the pew, waving a sprig of holly like a baton.

And then Elizabeth Ashdown arrived.

She swept down the aisle in midnight-blue velvet and diamonds that knew their worth. Heads turned. Murmurs followed. She gave a small, knowing smile, enough to seem gracious, not enough to deny awareness. Charlotte followed discreetly, carrying a prayer book and a look that said, please, Lord, no theatrics today.

From the front, David caught sight of them and managed not to sigh aloud. There was something in the way she moved through the church, confident, controlled, with just the faintest air of mischief, that always unsettled him. She was a living parable: beautiful, divisive, and entirely unrepentant.

By the third carol, *Once in Royal David's City*, something began stirring at the back. A rustle, a whisper, a faint metallic ping. David knew that sound—the distinctive chime of Montague in possession of an idea.

"Not now," hissed Beryl Wills from beside him.

"But it's showtime!" Montague whispered, eyes gleaming. "We're due our finale!"

"This is the midnight service, not a matinee."

"I promised a spectacle!"

"Then close your mouth," said Beryl.

From the front, David didn't hear every word, but he felt the tremor of danger ripple up the aisle. Parish instinct, like weather sense. Something was about to go wrong. He prayed it would at least be original.

After the readings, the church settled into that rare and precious quiet, the kind that feels like waiting rather than absence. David climbed the pulpit steps, sermon in hand. Below him stretched a sea of faces: familiar, curious, affectionate, and faintly suspicious.

He began simply. "Christmas," he said, "is God's most uncoordinated miracle. Nothing went to plan. No room, no rehearsal, no choir practice. Only love, arriving anyway."

The congregation leaned in. The candles trembled. For a moment, everything held still. Then a small *pop* echoed through the nave. A heartbeat later, silver glitter burst across the air.

Gasps. Laughter. Coughs. A child squealed, "Snow inside!"

Montague stood frozen at the back, holding the smoking remains of his banned glitter cannon. His hair sparkled like a disco nativity.

"Artistic exuberance," he croaked.

Beryl smacked him on the arm. "Idiot exuberance!"

David shut his eyes briefly. "As I was saying," he continued, brushing sparkles off his sermon, "light breaks through the dark—sometimes rather literally."

Laughter rippled through the pews. Even Mrs Dawson cracked a smile, though she immediately wrote *"disciplinary note"* in her margin. The tension broke, replaced by something better—joy, unrestrained and thoroughly human.

By the time they reached *Hark! The Herald Angels Sing*, the air still shimmered faintly. The choir sang as if competing with heaven. Montague hummed along with operatic abandon until Beryl silenced him with a glare. Elizabeth's voice joined in quietly, warm and clear, her eyes fixed on the altar.

As the final verse ended, the candles were lit for *Silent Night*. The congregation's faces glowed gold and still, softened by the shared peace of exhaustion. Children slept against parents' shoulders. The choir's voices floated like breath on glass. Even Mrs Dawson's clipboard drooped slightly in reverence.

Elizabeth's gaze found David's. For a heartbeat, something unspoken passed between them, not flirtation, exactly, but recognition. They were both performers today, each holding up grace for others to see, even while carrying their own unrest.

When the last note faded, David gave the blessing. "Go in peace," he said. "And if you can't manage peace, at least take the joy with you. It's lighter to carry."

The congregation laughed softly, applauded the choir, and began to spill out into the snow. Gloves found hands; scarves were pulled tighter; good wishes were exchanged like currency. Elizabeth approached the vicar at the porch, her smile polite and unreadable. "Well done, Canon. You've managed to turn catastrophe into theology. That's quite a feat."

"It's the only one I can claim," he said.

She handed him a small parcel, neatly wrapped in white paper and silver ribbon. "A Christmas peace offering."

"You didn't have to…"

"I did," she interrupted gently. "If only to stop the rumour that I'm giving you jewellery again."

He raised an eyebrow. "Ah, the infamous cufflinks."

"Still making their rounds?"

"Like wandering relics."

"Well," she said, "this one is entirely innocent. Open it with a sherry later. That's when the truth looks prettiest."

She smiled, nodded, and swept out into the snow, her perfume lingering faintly like a memory.

The churchyard was hushed beneath its quilt of snow. Lanterns flickered; footsteps whispered; breath hung in the cold air like smoke. The sun above was deliberate and the sky blue as the sea. Near the gate, Daisy waited, clutching her hymn book. Her halo of curls caught the lamplight. "Lovely sermon," she said. "Even the glitter."

He chuckled. "That part wasn't authorised by the liturgy."

"I think it should be," she said. "Sometimes God needs a bit of sparkle."

He looked at her, seeing the quiet steadiness beneath her shy humour. "You're probably right."

She hesitated. "Will you come to the village breakfast tomorrow?"

"Wouldn't miss it," he said. "Though I may sit far from the mistletoe."

Her laughter turned to mist in the cold air. "Merry Christmas, Canon."

"And to you, Daisy."

As she walked away, her blue scarf trailing behind her, he watched the church windows glowing warm with the striking sun and felt something he couldn't name—gratitude, perhaps, or grace disguised as exhaustion.

Back inside, the church was emptying. Mrs Dawson gathered abandoned service sheets with the air of a general after battle. Montague was attempting to sweep glitter from the nave, though each sweep seemed to redistribute it. Gerald Davies locked the choir vestry with a sigh.

David helped extinguish the last of the candles. As he did, he noticed one still burning stubbornly at the side of the altar, a small flame, crooked but bright. He left it. Some lights, he thought, weren't meant to be tidied away.

Later, in the vicarage, the silence pressed softly. The fire crackled, and the old clock marked midday with an uneven chime. He hung up his coat, loosened his collar, and sat at his desk, where the golden cufflinks still rested beside his sermon notes.

He hesitated before unwrapping Elizabeth's parcel. The paper was smooth, the ribbon tied with maddening precision. Inside was a small silver bell, delicate but weighty, its clapper engraved with a single word: *Peace*.

He smiled, touched and troubled in equal measure, and set it beside the cufflinks. The two gleamed together, gold and silver, initials and silence, two halves of a story still unfolding.

He opened his sermon again and added one final line, almost as a benediction to himself:

*Peace doesn't arrive because we're ready for it. It arrives precisely because we aren't.*

He underlined the sentence once, slowly. Outside, the bells of St Michael's began their uneven peal—off-time, off-key, and utterly perfect. The sound rolled over the snowbound roofs, through the sleepy Christmas village, and into the corners of every house that had somehow made it to Christmas intact.

David sat listening until the echoes faded. Then, with a sigh that was half prayer, half laughter, he whispered, "Well, Lord... they're still ringing." And in the silence that followed, it almost sounded as though the village itself answered. A breath of wind through the eaves, a distant crack of frost, the faint chime of the little silver bell on his desk, all blending into something like joy. An early night he thought, the one he'd promised himself for weeks.

Morning on St Stephen's day came softly, the snow still deep and bright. The village stirred slowly, blinking its way back into consciousness after the long night of carols, chaos, and candlelight. The first sound came from the bell tower, late, lopsided, and proud of itself for still functioning.

In the church hall, the scent of frying bacon and instant coffee was already filling the air. The annual Christmas breakfast, St Michael's most disorderly tradition, was under way.

Beryl Wills was in command. "Plates on the left, tea on the right, and anyone who says the sausages are burnt can make their own."

Mrs Dawson, miraculously unarmed by clipboard, was ladling porridge into bowls. "We should say grace," she announced.

"We did," said Montague, who had appointed himself chief taster. "Three times, while you weren't looking."

Daisy arrived wrapped in a scarf the size of a duvet, cheeks pink from the cold. "Merry Christmas!" she called.

"Merry chaos," said Beryl. "Canon not here yet?"

"Probably sermonising the frost," said Montague. "Or repenting the glitter."

"More likely cleaning it off his dog collar," Daisy replied.

When David finally arrived, still looking faintly dazed from the night before, the room broke into applause. Someone struck up *We Wish You a Merry Christmas* on a recorder, and someone else, probably Montague, threw a handful of tinsel like confetti.

"Morning," said David, brushing sparkle from his sleeve. "I see we're observing the usual liturgy of carbohydrates."

"Breakfast is the holiest meal," declared Beryl. "Nothing else forgives as quickly."

He smiled. "Amen to that."

They found him a chair, though it wobbled dangerously. The table before him was a masterpiece of parish improvisation with mismatched plates, fairy lights, a poinsettia already drooping from the heat. The food was hearty, the conversation louder than the hymn that followed.

Mrs Dawson leaned forward. "Canon, I must say, that sermon yesterday...inspired. The bit about peace arriving when we're not ready for it."

"Thank you," he said. "It seemed appropriate."

"And very true," she added. "We certainly weren't ready for that glitter."

"Or for Montague's encore," said Beryl.

Montague smiled beatifically. "Art resists containment."

"Art," said Beryl, "nearly set the pulpit on fire."

They all laughed. The morning light poured through the hall windows, turning the air to gold. For once, the village seemed perfectly content—no scandals, no speculation, just warmth and the faint crackle of the urn.

Charlotte appeared in the doorway, looking as though she had already been up for hours. "Mrs Ashdown sends her apologies," she announced. "She's hosting lunch for the estate staff."

"Of course she is," said Beryl. "Running on champagne and self-control."

Charlotte smiled faintly. "And she asked me to deliver these." She handed David a small parcel of mince pies wrapped in linen. "She said to tell you they're her grandmother's recipe, very traditional."

"Dangerously so," murmured David, but he accepted them with a smile. Inside the linen was a sprig of holly tied with silver thread. Beneath it, a small note in Elizabeth's elegant hand: *For later. Even miracles need breakfast first.*

Montague leaned over his shoulder. "A secret message from the lady of the manor! The plot thickens."

"So does the porridge," muttered Beryl.

They ate and laughed and told stories that grew taller by the minute. Daisy recounted how the donkey costume had been salvaged from the roof; Mrs Dawson swore she had seen an angel over the church (it turned out to be the weathervane). Montague, not to be outdone, insisted he had been asked to produce next year's Nativity *"in the style of Andrew Lloyd Webber."*

"Not again," said Beryl. "I've still got glitter in my shoes."

"That's the spirit of Christmas," he said. "It lingers."

When breakfast was done, the tables were cleared with surprising efficiency. People began to drift home, scarves trailing, calling good wishes through the snow. Outside, the morning sun turned the frost to diamonds.

Daisy lingered by the door, watching as David helped stack chairs. "You really should sit down," she said. "You've been up half the night."

"So have you."

"Yes, but I'm younger and fuelled by sugar."

"Ah," he said. "The secret of sainthood."

She smiled. "More like survival. You know, I think everyone needed last night—even with the glitter."

He nodded slowly. "Especially with it."

As the hall emptied, he stepped outside. The village lay hushed, white and shining. Smoke curled from chimneys. The air smelt of pine and toast. From somewhere near the pub came the sound of laughter and a badly tuned carol.

He walked back toward the church. The doors stood open, candles still flickering inside from the night before. The light through the stained glass painted the floor in soft colour. He sat in a pew, the silence pressing close, kind rather than heavy.

He took the little silver bell from his pocket and held it up to the morning light. It chimed once, a sound small enough to be missed, yet perfect enough to stay. He set it beside the cufflinks on the altar rail. Together they caught the sun, gold, silver, peace, mystery all the tangled meanings of Christmas.

Behind him came a voice. "You left the best line out of your sermon."

He turned. Elizabeth stood in the doorway, her fur collar dusted with snow.

"Oh?" he said. "Which line was that?"

"The one about how love survives everything," she said. "Even gossip."

He smiled. "I thought I'd save that for next year."

"Wise," she said. "The village needs a rest."

They stood together for a moment, the sunlight pooling around them. Then she reached out and touched the silver bell. "Peace," she murmured. "It suits you."

"And you," he said softly.

She met his eyes, amused and unflinching. "Careful, Canon. That sounds like a confession."

"Occupational hazard," he replied.

She laughed, low, warm, unmistakably human for her. "Merry Christmas, David."

"And to you, Elizabeth."

She turned to go, her footsteps light against the stone. When the door closed behind her, the air seemed to hold her presence for a while—scent, laughter, something unfinished but gentle.

Outside, the bell tower gave a final chime, almost in tune. From the hill beyond, children's voices, shrill, joyful, untidy as hope, carried through the cold.

David stood a moment longer in the quiet church. Then he gathered his notes, his peace, and his impossible village, and whispered the only prayer that felt honest.

"Thank you, Lord… for the glitter."

And with that, St Michael's began another St Stephen's Day, flawed, faithful, and gloriously alive.

# Chapter Eight
## Post-Christmas Peace (27 December)

Frost stitched lace along the church roof; the bells lay exhausted after their holiday labours, and even the carved angels looked as if they were nursing hangovers of incense and goodwill. The nave of St Michael's still smelled faintly of pine and wax and humanity, a mixture of prayer, gossip, and polish that had seeped into the stones over the long Advent weeks. Outside, the world had quietened into that curious stillness that follows festivity: snow dulled the lanes, smoke curled from chimneys, and the village, collectively, had the look of people recovering from generosity.

In the vicarage kitchen Canon David Thomlinson sat with toast, tea, and the unaccustomed luxury of silence. The range murmured companionably, the old clock stuttered through its minutes, and the kettle, for once, was not being asked to solve anyone's spiritual crisis. For the first time in months nothing seemed to require his opinion, signature, or presence. He toyed with the idea that this might be what peace actually felt like, a little underwhelming but blessedly steady.

The knock at the side door came precisely when the notion began to feel dangerous. He smiled at the ceiling. "And so it begins again."

Daisy Rivers stood on the step, her cheeks red with cold and a basket balanced on one arm beneath a cloth printed with holly and small, improbable robins. "Breakfast delivery," she said, stepping into the warmth. "From the choir. Mrs Dawson thought you'd forget to eat now that you've nothing left to sermonise about."

"I'll take that as pastoral concern," he said, ushering her toward the table. "Does it contain absolution or carbohydrates?"

"Both." She uncovered scones, cherry jam, and a slab of butter stabbed with a sprig of rosemary. "Gerald says it's symbolic. I say it's garnish."

"Symbolism always tastes better with dairy," said David, setting out plates. They ate companionably, the sound of spreading and sipping filling the comfortable gaps where conversation wasn't needed.

The small silver bell Elizabeth Ashdown had given him glinted beside the teapot, its thread tucked neatly under to keep it from rolling. Next to it lay the gold cufflinks, their mysterious initials still promising more gossip than gospel. Daisy's eyes went to them immediately.

"So, they weren't yours after all?"

"No. They've travelled farther than most missionaries."

"Will you ever find out who D and E are?"

"I think I already have," he said, and smiled into his tea.

Her eyebrow arched. "Elizabeth Ashdown and…?"

"Discretion," he interrupted gently. "It's one of the sacraments round here."

"That and tea."

"Exactly that order."

For a while they sat in companionable quiet. The vicarage had the hush of a theatre after the audience has gone home; you could still feel the echo of performance in the walls. Finally David said, "You sang well on Christmas Eve."

"Thank you. I think the glitter improved the acoustics."

"It improved the theology," he replied. "Every parish needs a miracle they can vacuum."

Daisy laughed, gathering her scarf. "I'd better go. Mrs Dawson's planning a debrief that will masquerade as a hymn rehearsal."

"Tell her I said we're triumphantly unscathed."

"I'll tell her we're triumphantly *contained*." She hesitated at the door. "Happy Christmas, Canon."

He nodded. "And to you, Daisy."

When she had gone, the quiet returned, gentler now, less absolute. He cleared the cups, ran a cloth across the table, and paused with his hand on the silver bell. The word engraved beneath his fingers, *Peace*, seemed faintly amused by its own optimism.

By noon, peace had unravelled in the usual way. The annual *post-Christmas luncheon* at Ashdown Hall waited, and ignoring an invitation from Elizabeth Ashdown was not merely impolite, it was futile. The card had arrived with the kind of phrasing that sounded like permission but wasn't.

The road to the Hall wound through fields still sugar-dusted from Boxing Day frost. Smoke from distant cottages rose in patient spirals, children tobogganed on biscuit tins down the mill slope; and the sea, visible between hedgerows, glittered like something remembering how to be cold. David tightened his scarf, told himself he was going in a pastoral capacity, and failed to believe it.

Ashdown Hall gleamed at the top of its drive, every window alight, every archway wreathed in greenery that had somehow survived three days of parties. The front doors opened as he approached, revealing Charlotte Penry with her notebook and the serenity of a woman who had faced greater crises armed only with a pencil.

"Canon," she said, with a warmth that was half relief. "We're just about ready. Mrs Ashdown insists on calling it *a simple luncheon.*"

"Which, I assume, means I should brace myself."

"Quite." She smiled. "If you'd be so good as to follow me before she rearranges the seating again."

The dining room was an opera in progress. Sunlight bounced from glass and silver; the fire in the grate whispered like applause. Elizabeth stood at the head of the table, magnificent in pale grey silk trimmed with fur that managed to look both extravagant and necessary. Around her clustered the chosen few: Beryl and David Wills; the Dawsons, already engaged in silent debate over the quality of the cutlery; Montague, whose paper crown tilted like a theological point; and, newly arrived, Daisy, seated halfway down to ensure conversational balance.

"Canon," Elizabeth said as he entered, "how obedient of you."

"I try to appear obedient in public," he said. "It disguises fatigue."

She gave that half-smile he had come to know, part amusement, part appraisal, and gestured him to the chair on her right.

"Shall we?" she said to the room at large, and the chorus of assent was both hungry and reverent.

"Canon," she added, "grace, if you would."

He stood. "For food, for friendship, and for the miracle that none of us perished of good intentions this season— Thanks be to God."

"Amen," murmured the table. The sound had the soft weariness of people who had already said many Amens that month.

Charlotte began to serve. The turkey, a leftover masterpiece reimagined as pie, steamed fragrantly; the vegetables shone with a buttery optimism that suggested Beryl's opinion would not be favourable. "They squeak," she observed, prodding a sprout. "Nothing edible should squeak."

Montague, meanwhile, was sketching the arrangement of the table in his notebook. "Inspiration," he murmured. "For next year's parish tableau. I'm thinking *Epiphany Re-imagined*."

"Don't," said Elizabeth, without turning her head. "The last time you re-imagined something, we lost a wise man to concussion."

Laughter shimmered briefly round the table before the conversation settled into its familiar rhythm—half gossip, half gratitude. Gerald Davies discussed hymn choices as if they were stock options; Mrs Dawson noted that attendance at the midnight service had *been "improving if one discounted the glitter episode"*. Beryl Wills pronounced the bread sauce "over educated."

David listened, answered where necessary, and let the tide of talk wash past. He had learned long ago that half the ministry of a village priest consisted of appearing gently amused.

The meal had just reached that pleasant lull between appetite and regret when the butler appeared, a solemn man who seemed personally affronted by the season. In his gloved hands was a silver tray bearing a single envelope.

"For you, madam," he intoned. "Delivered by hand."

Elizabeth lifted one perfectly drawn eyebrow. "On the twenty-seventh of December? Either a ghost of Christmas administration or a solicitor."

"From the family firm, ma'am. Something about a codicil."

The room brightened as if a fuse had been lit. Even the gravy paused.

"A codicil?" repeated Mrs Dawson, delight sharpening her vowels. "How very… legal."

"As in a will," Montague breathed, eyes gleaming. "At luncheon! Deliciously indecorous."

"Monty," murmured David, "your enthusiasm for mortality worries me."

Elizabeth slit the envelope with a small silver knife and read. Her expression barely changed, save for the faintest lift of amusement at the corner of her mouth.

"Well," she said lightly, "apparently I've inherited a bell."

"A bell?" Beryl repeated, halfway between interest and suspicion.

"Yes. A small silver one belonging originally to my great-grandmother. Lost for generations. It seems someone located it in a parish collection and returned it to the estate."

Across the table, David blinked. "A silver bell?"

Her eyes flicked to him over the rim of her glass. "Engraved, rather charmingly, with the word *Peace*."

For a moment the air between them shimmered with the sort of coincidence that feels suspiciously like design. Montague, sensing a plot, whispered "Providence!" and scribbled something theatrical in his notebook.

"How poetic," Mrs Dawson murmured.

"How implausible," said Beryl. "I call that divine mischief."

Elizabeth set the letter aside. "Family heirlooms," she said, "have an inconvenient habit of returning precisely when one has learned to live without them." She raised her glass. "To recovered things."

Glasses clinked, conversation cautiously resumed, and yet everyone seemed to listen harder, as if the story might continue without permission. The turkey tasted somehow more interesting. Even Montague, chastened, confined his commentary to sotto voce quotations from *The Bells of St Mary's*.

By the time pudding arrived, formidable, flaming, and brandied into obedience, the mood had lifted into that contented haze of shared absurdity. Gerald declared the custard *"redemptive."* Mrs Dawson forgave the glitter incident on the grounds of *"artistic exuberance."* Beryl discovered she quite liked squeaky sprouts after all.

"Canon," Elizabeth said suddenly, as if the thought had struck her mid-spoonful, "if one were to host a modest Epiphany concert, would that violate diocesan restraint?"

"Only if it features livestock or fire," he said.

"Then we shall call it *Lessons and Aftermath*," she replied, entirely straight-faced.

Charlotte leaned down to murmur something. A moment later she disappeared and returned carrying a small velvet box. Elizabeth tapped her fork against her glass; conversation obediently stilled.

"It seems," she announced, "that the season's final mystery can be put to rest." She opened the box and held up a pair of gold cufflinks. "These, it appears, were never stolen, gifted, or exchanged illicitly. The jeweller found them during his post-Christmas audit. A clerical error, proof that the Church has no monopoly on confusion."

A wave of relieved laughter swept the table, mixed with a little disappointment from those who secretly preferred scandal.

"So you may all relax," she continued. "The Canon and I are not engaged, eloping, or planning a limited-edition jewellery line, at least, not this year."

Montague groaned theatrically. "There goes my subplot."

Daisy laughed, the unguarded, bright sound of someone whose shoulders had finally dropped an inch. Mrs Dawson made a small note in the air as if to re-categorise the incident under *Innocuous but Promising.*

Elizabeth turned the cufflinks thoughtfully in her fingers and met David's eye. "There we are, Canon. Peace restored."

He inclined his head. "Chaos has its charm."

"So does closure," she said. "Though it rarely lasts."

"Nor should it," he replied. "We'd run out of sermons."

Coffee arrived. Crackers were pulled. Montague recited the joke about the vicar, the bishop, and the parrot; Beryl threw the hat at him in protest. The meal drifted toward its end in the easy, affectionate disarray of people who have decided to forgive each other until Lent.

The Wills left first, "bells to check," muttered Beryl, meaning leftovers. Gerald and Elinor followed, still bickering amiably about descants. Montague lingered to praise the acoustics of the pudding before Charlotte ushered him into the snow with quiet efficiency.

When the house finally exhaled, Elizabeth stood in the doorway of the drawing room, a figure carved in silk and light. Beyond the windows the park lay silver and still; the ornamental lake had frozen into a sheet of glass that reflected the pale sky like a sigh.

Charlotte returned from dispatching the last guest. "You're quiet, ma'am."

"I'm deciding whether to take up bell-ringing," said Elizabeth.

"Please don't," said Charlotte.

They exchanged a smile that acknowledged entire years of shared endurance.

"The Canon looks tired," said Elizabeth after a moment, watching the shadow of him crossing the courtyard. "But taller."

"That'll be the peace," said Charlotte. "It's terribly good for posture."

Elizabeth laughed, softly, genuinely, and turned back toward the fire.

David found his coat, thanked Charlotte, and took his leave with a small blessing that lingered like warmth in the hall long after the door had closed behind him. Outside, dusk was beginning to blue the snow, and the village lay spread beneath him, roofs glinting, chimneys exhaling.

From the upper windows of Ashdown Hall drifted the faint sound of laughter, and the unmistakable clatter of Montague rediscovering his gloves with operatic despair.

The road home felt shorter than usual. The air smelled of frost and roast potatoes. In the distance he could hear the Red Lion's door slamming and a baritone attempting *Good King Wenceslas* in what might generously be called a key.

At the lychgate he paused and looked back. A single window high in the Hall still glowed. Behind the glass stood Elizabeth, one hand resting against it, the other touching the diamond at her throat. She saw him looking, gave the smallest nod, not farewell, not invitation, simply acknowledgment, and then withdrew from the light. He smiled, that mild, private smile that belonged to no congregation, and tipped his hat.

The village had entered that sacred hush that comes after laughter — when even dogs sense the holiness of leftovers. The Red Lion brimmed with consolation and bad carols; the churchyard lay peaceful beneath its new dusting of snow.

Later, by his fireside, he opened the worn notebook that held the detritus of the season: sermons, shopping lists, reminders to visit Mrs Jenkins about her grandson who had set fire to the Advent wreath "by mistake but successfully." On a clean page he wrote, slowly and deliberately:

*For all our noise, confusion, and small scandals, love has still arrived, inconvenient, uninvited, and entirely on time.*

He read the line twice, decided it could bear the weight of truth, and closed the book.

The little silver bell lay on the mantel beside the cufflinks. He lifted it, rang it once. The note was clear and calm, the kind of sound that didn't need to prove itself.

He placed it down again, banked the fire, and watched the last flames gather into the shape of contentment. Outside, the snow began once more, hesitant, then steady, then generous, and through it the bells of St Michael's found their uneven peal: off-time, off-key. Utterly perfect.

Somewhere between the vicarage hearth and the sleeping Hall, the village exhaled. The snow fell soft as forgiveness, and for one long breath, St Michael's was, improbably, undeniably, at peace.

## About the Author

**James Thomas** writes about the charm, chaos, and quiet miracles of village life, those small English worlds where scandal brews as easily as tea and faith is best served with a sense of humour.

A lifelong observer of human nature (and parish notices), he brings warmth, wit, and an affectionate eye for the absurd to every page. *A Country Parish Christmas: Mistletoe and Mayhem* is the first festive story set in the world of St Michael's, a place where nothing ever quite goes to plan, yet everything somehow turns out all right in the end.

When not writing, James can usually be found with a cup of tea (or a glass of Doxy Gin), in a church pew, or wondering how on earth the flower rota became controversial again.

Find out more, and join the congregation of readers, at **www.jthomasbooks.co.uk**

## Coming Soon from James Thomas
*A Country Parish: A Parish Affair*
*(Book Two in the A Country Parish Series)*

## Scandal never rests, even after Christmas.
The snow has melted, but the gossip hasn't.
As spring approaches, St Michael's prepares for its next great drama, a missing ledger, a whisper about the Ashdown estate, and a sermon that might reveal more truth than anyone expected.

Canon David Thomlinson faces new tests of faith, friendship, and temptation, while Elizabeth Ashdown discovers that reputation can be both armour and weapon. And somewhere among the hymns, hats, and half-truths, one secret threatens to pull the village apart.

## Excerpt from Chapter One — Sunday Best
## Chapter One — Sunday Best

The bells of St Michael's Minster could be heard long before you saw the church itself. They rolled across the headland and rattled the hedgerows, bounced off the ashlar of the Ashdown estate, then slipped down through the village like a reminder from the past that the present still owed it courtesies. The sound made dogs lift their heads and shop doors pause on their hinges, and it also had the irritating habit (so Mrs Dawson observed) of exposing the late.

Canon David Thomlinson stood in the porch, cope lifted by the sea breeze as if it meant to sail him off the step. Today he wore his best: a heavy brocade chasuble, a gold-embroidered stole laid exactly, and atop them, a cope that flared with theatrical confidence. High Church liturgy, in David's view, was part theology, part stagecraft, and wholly necessary in a village that judged sincerity by the weight of the brass.

At his side hovered Adam Stewart, Master of Ceremonies, a man whose clipboard had toppled empires in his head if not in reality. He bore the permanent frown of someone gravely disappointed by other people's angles.

"Thurifer's late," Adam murmured, eyes on the lychgate. "And the candles are uneven. Again. I told young Thomas to carry the cross, he's got the height—but his mother insists he serves coffee instead, which shows you where priorities lie."

"Perhaps," David said, "her theology is caffeinated."

Adam did not laugh. Adam rarely allowed himself the luxury.

A rustle of cassocks and the faint chime of chains announced the serving team: Lily Evans, twelve and fierce, swinging the thurible as if she were certain smoke could fix anything; behind her, twins Matthew and Luke Price, solemn junior pallbearers for their own nerves; and, bearing the cross, Thomas Reed, promoted after a diplomatic incident involving candle wax and a hymn book. Adam flowed among them, nudging, aligning, lowering an elbow here, raising a chin there, an anxious stage manager whooshing the saints.

Inside, the organ was already prowling. Montague Wraxall-Blythe, who dressed as though the Palladium had requested his presence for the Eucharist, let a ripple of sound test the rafters. He had the smile of a man with secrets and a registration marked *subtle* that he had never used. In the chancel, Gerald Davies tapped a baton against the music stand with doomed optimism. At his shoulder, Elaine—soprano, spouse, and necessary corrective, wore the expression of a woman who knew exactly how much optimism could be afforded before it became farce.

In the front pew, Mrs Elinor Dawson had installed her hat (minor cathedral) and handbag (likely containing the Nicene Creed and four emergency policies) with proprietary finality. Two rows back, Helen Walters took up her quiet post by the flower fund tin, the cool gaze of a retired policewoman measuring the weight of every coin. Gareth Jones, ex-army and now churchwarden, surveyed the aisle as if planning a landing; Janice Williams, his colleague, had the easy calm of a teacher who could calm a gale with a hand on a shoulder.

The Ashdown's arrived with the hush that follows a change of wind. Lady Margaret moved as if the nave had been arranged for her; Hugh, watch checking, wore the patience of a man who had taught himself to be discreetly bored. Amelia slipped beside her mother, fingers already greyed by graphite—while Charlotte hovered half a step behind as if she preferred the threshold to the centre. Edward, mercifully, had not yet materialised.

And then the air sharpened. Elizabeth Ashdown entered without ceremony and with all of it. You felt her before you saw her; then the cane clicked once, and the front pews sat up an inch. Her glance took in the porch, the vestments, the line of acolytes; the smallest nod declared the place acceptable to God and to her, in that order which she would not wish to see reversed.

"Canon," she said, voice as clean as cut glass, "do try not to set fire to anything I paid for."

"Only hearts, Mrs Ashdown," David replied lightly.

"Mm. Cheaper," she observed, and moved to her seat, leaving behind the faintest thread of lavender and the question of whether you had been complimented or warned.

The hymn number turned; Adam raised his hand; Lily's thurible swung a sunlit arc; and Montague launched the opening bars with the conviction of a man christening a ship. The procession gathered itself, cross, candles, smoke, choir, clergy—and the congregation straightened, as if the tide itself had appeared at the west door. David bowed at the step. Fabric breathed, the sanctuary lamp flickered like an obedient star, and the words of the rite found their old groove.

Elaine took the First Reading and delivered it like a stern chat with Saint Paul about punctuality. The Second Reading belonged to Amelia; her voice, unexpectedly gentle, made the text sound briefly as though it had been written to her alone. Adam, hearing the unshowy beauty of it, made a neat tick on his list and allowed himself a private smile.

David sang the Gospel, book lifted, acolytes bracketing him in a halo of candlelight. The incense rose enthusiastically—Lily was generous, and momentarily swallowed Mrs Dawson to the shoulders. Her cough emerged from the cloud like a theological position.

His sermon was called *The Ties That Bind* and managed the trick of not naming anyone while causing several people to examine their shoes.

"Community," he began, "is a word we fling like confetti and then forget to sweep up. It's not just shared space; it's shared weight. It is history, yes, and duty, yes, and occasionally scandal, which is simply history with better gossip."

Mrs Dawson nodded vigorously, missing the subtext by choice.

"In a place like ours, the threads can chafe," David continued. "We tug. We test. We sometimes fray. And when that happens, it's the unglamorous work, the small apologies, the quiet kindnesses, the patient listening, that holds."

Lady Margaret maintained sculpted stillness; Gerald adjusted a hymn book he had already adjusted; Elaine arched one perfectly honed brow. At the back, Mark, new to the village, old in the art of not being noticed, let a smile move briefly at the corner of his mouth. The sight disturbed David more than it should have, which he ignored with professional skill.

At the Peace, the parish resumed its familiar choreography of polite warfare. Mrs Dawson's handshake conveyed absolution and policy updates; Elaine's conveyed a weapon she chose not to use. Gareth saluted two strangers; Janice rescued him with a nod. Helen's slight bow to David contained, somehow, both appreciation and an agenda item.

The offertory procession wavered and recovered like all living things. The twins leaned their candles towards the flowers in a way that made Adam whiten; he effected a mid-aisle rescue so smooth the congregation mistook it for planned dignity. Daisy, seamstress, parish salvation, spotted a loose braid on the green chasuble and consigned it to her mental mending list; John, her husband and the verger, winced at the sixteenth-century brass ring doing duty as a temporary coaster for the sacristy keys.

At the altar, the great prayer uncoiled and steadied him. His mind might wander to the small cruelties of the hall, the heavier presences of the study, Sarah's tablets near the kettle, the letter in his desk whose fold remembered a bishop's hand—but here the words sat like stones in a wall, properly placed and bearing weight.

Communion arrived as it always did, like small weather. Lily attempted to extinguish a candle by glaring at it. The parish flowed up, knelt, rose, flowed back, and the rustle of kneelers gave the old stone its polite applause. Lady Margaret knelt with perfect spine; Charlotte let her eyelids fall, not dramatically but with relief. Elizabeth received, rose, and, passing David, murmured, "You did not waste the congregation's attention, Canon. Cherish the rarity."

# A Country Parish Christmas: Mistletoe and Mayhem

The final hymn struggled in Montague's hands, which delighted him. Gerald's baton brought it to heel with a visible sigh. The blessing rang clean, the dismissal landed, and St Michael's shifted into its second service: tea, chairs, and the sacrament of saying what one really thought.

The hall had the smell of every village hall: steam, biscuits, lavender hand cream, and a floor polish that claimed in four languages to be non-slip. The urn breathed like an old horse. Gareth's traffic-flow rope was ignored with respectful unanimity. Helen placed the flower fund tin with mathematical exactness; she could hear a sixpence sulking.

"Such a brave colour for the countryside," Mrs Dawson told Jackie Ashcroft, intercepting her at the custard creams like a border guard. "Of course, one should always express oneself—even if the hedge objects."

Jackie smiled politely and held her paper cup like a passport. Martyn hovered beside her until Gareth relieved him with a tutorial on correct chair-stacking (weight distribution, risk assessment, heritage protection).

Elaine cornered Lady Margaret with sugar tongs and courtesy. "Splendid turnout. Remarkable, really, given Edward's... schedule."

Lady Margaret's smile could have cut glass. "We Ashdown's always support the parish, dear. Publicly and privately."

"Then your generosity is noted," Elaine replied sweetly. "One never knows when notes might be needed."

At the back wall, Beryl Wills watched the ebb and flow with a smile set to low. In front of her, David Wills lectured Malcolm Wilson, treasurer, long suffering, on the true tempo of the recessional hymn and on how modern bell ringers lacked a grasp of metronomic duty once taught to real men and the occasional woman. Malcolm tried on interest and returned it to the peg.

Montague had stationed himself near the urn to inflict theory upon the still. "You see," he told a small captive audience, "the nineteenth-century glass contains a Masonic code, or possibly a Romanesque weather forecast obscured by Victorian anxiety, one never knows with donors." John the verger leaned in, delighted to correct a date by thirty-two years, whereupon Montague thanked him flamboyantly and did not change his mind.

Helen remained at her post by the tin, the kind of vigil that made guilt itch. She could feel when coins arrived in pairs and left in threes.

David threaded through the conversations with the ease of a man skilled at listening to what people meant and replying to what they said. He noticed Adam, hovering in the doorway with a sheaf of notes.

"Canon," Adam began with the relief of someone about to hand over contraband, "I've made a few observations on the liturgy. Minor adjustments, naturally. We must never concede to chaos."

"I'll read every word," David said, which was kind and untrue in equal measure.

Near the hatch, Gerald and David Wills were still litigating the recessional. "If the choir followed the beat," Gerald insisted, "there would have been no lag."

"If the beat were where you conduct it," David Wills replied, "they would have found it."

Beryl's smile flickered, then steadied again.

Sarah's absence had not gone unremarked. "Not herself," Mrs Dawson confided to Janice, at a volume calibrated for two pews. "Such a shame. One does hope the vicarage has a reliable kettle."

David's smile went courteous and hollow for a beat, then reset. Without quite deciding to, he found himself beside Mark, who had achieved a posture of relaxed observation on the windowsill.

"Your parishioners are quite the ensemble," Mark said quietly, amusement hanging off the words like a ribbon.

"You should see them at the fete," David replied. "There's bunting."

"I plan to."

The current between them was brief and definite. David stepped back into safer waters, which still felt like a risk.

Helen's arrival at his elbow was as discreet as a warning can be. "We've a shortfall in the flower fund," she said, voice low.

"How short?"

"Short enough to have a pattern."

"Bring the ledger Monday."

Her nod said she already had.

The tide of parishioners receded with the usual reluctance. The urn sighed. Chairs stacked. Adam rescued a hymn book from a life of anarchy. Mrs Dawson complimented the tea while implying it had sinned. Elaine consigned Montague's jazz aspirations to the outer darkness for the Sanctus, then set about recruiting two altos with the benevolent menace of a sainted head girl.

By the time David returned to the nave, the quiet had crept back onto the stone. The cold in the air made the incense last longer. He moved through the church as through a house after guests have gone, setting things right: a straightened missal, a candle wick trimmed, a brass candlestick remembered by his hand. He paused in the Lady Chapel and traced the edge of a candlestick with his thumb, the cool metal anchoring him.

The morning replayed itself: Sarah's absence like a note withheld; Mrs Dawson's comment dressed as concern; the glance from Mark that had landed a fraction too close; Amelia's reading; Elizabeth's economy of approval. He told himself the parish had weathered worse. He wondered whether he believed himself.

A tap at the vestry window startled him. Helen stood there, ledger raised in one hand, expression like weather on its way. She mouthed, *It's worse than I thought.* He nodded and gestured to the clock: later.

He extinguished the altar candles, slow and careful. The sanctuary lamp kept its small flame. He looked up at the crucifix and let a breath go.

"You understand," he murmured, half prayer, half jest.

The last lock clicked. The porch opened to a sunlight that behaved as if nothing difficult had ever happened here. The churchyard stones, smug with history, warmed their faces. Somewhere beyond the wall, the sea threw itself at the shore again and again, as if trying to remember something it couldn't quite recall.

But beneath the calm, the ground was shifting. And somewhere between the ledger on Helen's arm and the look in Elizabeth Ashdown's eye, David felt the parish deciding to test its threads.

## A Country Parish: A Parish Affair — coming 2026

Keep up with new releases and updates from **J. Thomas** at **www.jthomasbooks.co.uk**

## Acknowledgements

Writing about village life is rather like joining a bell ringers' practice — you start with good intentions, end up tangled, and somehow make a joyful noise, anyway.

My thanks to everyone who inspired, endured, or accidentally resembled the residents of St Michael's (I assure you, any resemblance is coincidental — but do check your parish newsletter just in case).

To the readers who've followed from the first peal to the final hymn, thank you for laughing, guessing, and forgiving the glitter.

To friends and family, for patience, cake, and reminders that reality can be even stranger than fiction — you are the heart behind the chaos.

And to Hilary — thank you.
For the tea, the thick chocolate biscuits, and the long conversations about parish perils while looking out over sheep-dotted fields.

Your generous literary eye has improved this book in more ways than you know, and your friendship has made the writing of it a far warmer process.

And to those who keep real churches, halls, and hearts open at Christmas: this story belongs to you.

— JamesThomas

Made in United States
North Haven, CT
18 December 2025